I0822665

BLACKENED ROOTS

AN ANTHOLOGY OF THE UNDEAD

Edited by

NICOLE GIVENS KURTZ AND TONIA RANSOM

CONTENTS

COPYRIGHT NOTICE

Hardcover ISBN: 979-8-9873795-9-2

Paperback ISBN: 979-8-9873795-8-5

EBook ISBN: 979-8-9873795-7-8

Cover Art Design by Sean Hill

Pencils and Lettering by Krishna Balram

Proofreader: Nicole Givens Kurtz

Publisher: Mocha Memoirs Press

OTHER MOCHA MEMOIRS HORROR ANTHOLOGY TITLES

SLAY: Stories of the Vampire Noire edited by Nicole Givens Kurtz

Black Magic Women edited by Sumiko Saulson

In the Bloodstream: An Anthology of Dark Fantasy and Horror edited by Eden Royce

Sisters of the Wild Sage: A Weird Western Collection by Nicole Givens Kurtz

Ghosts, Gears, and Grimoires edited by Rie Sheridan Rose

The Grotesquerie: 22 Horror Stories by Women edited by Eden Royce

RECIPE FOR A ZOMBIE

EDEN ROYCE

In these days of mass-produced everything, sometimes it's a joy to focus on the handcrafting of one special item. One you can dedicate yourself to perfecting. Trends in zombies have moved to armies of chemically-created mindless flesh-eaters—a far cry from their origins.

The *zonbi* was born in Haiti, where the intended was specially and lovingly chosen. Once selected, they were molded in an artisan fashion where the practitioner accepted the time required as inseparable from the end result: one person, bound to do their bidding.

While zombies are created with Vodoun and aren't usually in my repertoire as a hoodooienne, this recipe is a fusion of both magics that yields a minion anyone can treasure.

Preparation time: 30 minutes **"Cooking" time:** 24 hours
Difficulty: Easy **Makes:** one

As with all magic recipes, the smart practitioner is prepared. Wear comfortable shoes with traction in case the need to move quickly arises. Bring your resolve as well, because once you've begun, there is no going back.

But if you've decided to take on this recipe, it's likely you already know that.

Ingredients:

- your intended
- lockable room
- one handful of Narcissus powder
- pinto coffin*
- white paint or chalk
- salt
- seven black candles (lard or beeswax is best, but soy will do)
- matches or lighter
- cast iron pan (optional)

*If you do not have a pinto coffin, which is cheap pine nailed together, a trunk or crate or any kind of breathable container will suffice.

Directions:

Remove coffin lid.

. . .

Isolate your intended with a casual invitation to your locale. If you are already on intimate terms, all the easier. If not, the offer of a cup of coffee or a glass of wine is a tried and true ruse.

Administer the powder. Some recipes will tell you to blow it in the intended's face, but this isn't a requirement. The object is to get it into the bloodstream quickly, so find the closest and most accessible mucous membrane.

STEP BACK. Your intended will likely have a brief moment of shock after exposure to the powder. After this, all bets are off! Your vict— intended may jerk, spasm, grab at you… any number of unpredictable things. This is where those high- traction shoes will come in handy. Get out of their way. They won't be able to get far. Soon, they'll crash to the floor.

This is the hard part. Keep your nerve. Remorse, tinged with horror at what you've done, may creep in and some may find their desire to continue will waver. Understandable when you see someone you know and/or love catatonic on the floor. Should you find yourself on the precipice at this step of the recipe, don't despair. This is where you must dig deep, beyond any shred of lingering sympathy, and pull on the real reasons you are making this recipe.

Are you furious that your subordinate has now become your boss?

Has someone you called friend been seen out with your heart's desire?

Or maybe you are like me... with a general misanthropy that pervades everything you do. Whatever your own personal reasons, find your purpose and clutch it tight. Let it propel you through the remainder of the task.

Do you have it?

Good. Moving on...

ONCE THE INTENDED CALMS, approach with the cast iron pan in hand. The powder should have done all of the work for you, but if they're not completely subdued and try to rise, hit them in the temple. Not too hard, or you may cause damage beyond repair. If you have the arm strength, a well-aimed punch will accomplish the same goal. Should the intended's bladder or bowels loosen, don't worry—this is normal. Move on to the next step and clean up later.

UNLOCK THE ROOM, lift or drag your intended inside and place them into prepared coffin. Paint your name over their head and heart. Close coffin and nail shut. Surround with salt. Place candles around the box in a clockwise direction and light each in order of placement. Seal room and leave undisturbed for 24 hours.

IMPORTANT: No peeking! Many a practitioner has been disappointed with the results because curiosity got the better of them. Ignore the scrabbling and scratching. Tidy up. Distract yourself. Have a hot bath and get some well-deserved rest.

. . .

The next day, unlock the door. Survey the room. If the ring of salt is undisturbed, enter and open the box. Your intended should be reclining inside, ready to do your will. Test by giving your zombie a simple instruction. Perhaps to smile or kiss your hand. If your zombie is able to complete these tasks with little effort, slowly incorporate more complicated commands or those your intended at one time found distasteful or beneath them.

Above all, enjoy your hard work!

INITIATION

MILTON J. DAVIS

Maria watched the horde through her battered binoculars, searching for the perfect one. This was the third mass they had encountered since morning. The smell of decaying flesh reached them despite the distance, carried by a stiff wind which heralded an approaching rainstorm. She shifted her attention to the gathering clouds, lightning flashes proceeding the distant rumbles.

"You see one?" Leo asked.

Maria shifted her attention back to the horde.

"Not yet," she replied.

The town had been ravaged by the undead before. Thinking beings would bypass it, but the hordes would sweep the same spots again and again.

Maria eyebrows rose over the binocular lens.

"Got one!"

She focused on a smaller undead. It was probably eight or nine years old when it transitioned. The condition of its clothes indicated it had been taken recently. Maria stopped identifying them by gender long ago. The more you removed their humanity, the easier it was to do what you had to do to survive.

"Let's go," Leo said.

He started the motorcycle as she forced her helmet down over her voluminous afro then climbed into the sidecar. Leo drove slowly, over the rough ground then accelerated when they reached the smoother asphalt. They covered half the distance before parking the bike. They were in no danger, but old habits were hard to break. Maria fished the shotgun from under their coats, and Leo grabbed the axe. They strolled across the patchwork of grass, weeds, and dirt as the undead entered the town. The creatures staggered in single file then separated, following the various streets branching from the main road.

The young one held back as if unsure, which was good for Leo and Maria. Maria opened the double barrel shotgun then inserted two buckshot shells. She crept closer until she was a meter away from it.

"Boo."

The undead turned and she pulled the trigger. The shot ripped through its head, sending decayed flesh and black blood everywhere. The headless creature tottered then fell forward.

Maria reloaded the shotgun as Leo strolled to the body.

"How much we need?" Maria asked.

"Not much."

Leo grabbed the undead's left arm and extended it. He chopped off the hand with one swing. It took three to cleave the arm at the elbow. He squatted before the body as Maria kept watch, picking up the arm then putting it into a silk-lined canvas bag.

"They're coming," Maria said. A gathering of undead walked toward them, blank eyes staring, deformed mouths open.

The duo strolled to the motorbike. Maria watched the group

come closer and she smirked. Leo started the bike, but Maria raised her hand.

"Wait," she said.

Leo frowned. "For what? We got what we came for."

"I want to see it work," she said.

Leo sighed then folded his arms on the bike handles. The undead came a few meters closer then stopped. They swayed in their unstable way, gazing around as if they could no longer see them. Then they turned away one by one, returning to the town.

Maria grinned. "Amazing." She hunkered down into the side car.

"Let's go."

* * *

It was raining when they reached the compound. The tower guards recognized them and opened the gate a few minutes before they arrived. Camp folk waved as they sloshed by to the command tent in the center of the town. Leo stopped before the entrance and Maria climbed out of the sidecar, the canvas bag containing the arm slung over her shoulder.

"I'll meet you at home," she said.

Leo nodded then drove away. Maria watched him and warmth passed through her despite the cold drizzle. She was lucky. Leo was a good man. They had been through so much together since The Change, circumstances that would have destroyed most couples. But they survived. They found the commune and were accepted. Now they were contributing to the community in the most important way.

When she entered the tent, she was greeted by the stern face of Gretchen Moore, head scientist. The sepia-colored clinic manager wore a dingy lab coat over her jeans and flannel shirt, her tight cross necklace barely visible. Maria threw up a lazy salute and Gretchen waved it off.

"Where's the package?" she said.

Maria handed her the bag. Gretchen opened it, looked inside then smiled.

"By Her Grace," she whispered. When she looked up, she radiated a reverent glow.

"You and Leo did an excellent job. I can see it's fresh. Did you watch the transformation?"

Maria barely hid her disgust.

"No. It was traveling with the Pollo Horde," she answered.

Gretchen hurried away, Maria close behind. They pushed through the canvas curtain into her lab. Maria was always amazed at how clean she kept the facility. Gretchen sat the appendage on the lab table then went to her storage cabinet and took out a med kit. She gave it to Maria.

"Make sure his vitals are good," she said.

"I will," Maria replied.

"You must be excited."

"Actually, I'm a little scared."

Gretchen looked at her with wide eyes.

"Scared? Why?"

Maria shrugged.

"Old habits I guess."

Gretchen carried the bag to the table then opened it. She took out the arm and admired it.

"You need to shake your doubts," Gretchen said. "Dr. Moore left us with an amazing legacy. It's terrible that he wasn't able to use it to save himself."

Gretchen closed her eyes then whispered a prayer. Everyone in the compound knew the story of Dr. Willis Moore and his revolutionary discovery. It was his serum that made life in the compound possible. It was also his search to improve his discovery that led him to become what he fought to destroy.

When Gretchen opened her eyes, the serious expression had returned.

"Make sure you check Barron's vitals. We need him in his best shape for Initiation."

"I will," Maria replied. "Thank you, Gretchen."

"No need to thank me. We are Tribe."

"We are Tribe," Maria repeated.

Maria left the med tent then hurried home. Leo's bike was parked out front, covered with the rain canvas. As she entered the tent, she saw her men sitting at the rusted folding table enjoying bowls of bone soup. Barron looked up and his face glowed.

"Mami!"

He jumped from her seat, then wrapped her in a crushing loving hug. He was almost as tall as Leo now, which made her happy and sad. She was gaining a healthy man but losing her boy.

"Let your mother go so she can eat," Leo said playfully.

They walked together to the table, separating to sit. The bone soup was warm and soothing.

"What did Gretchen say?" Leo asked.

"Everything is good," Maria replied. "Initiation is on schedule."

Barron's face dimmed; his smile replaced by a nervous scowl. Maria reached out and touched his hand.

"It's nothing to worry about," she said. "Everything will be fine."

"I'm not worried about that," Barron replied. "I'm nervous about the ceremony. I don't like crowds."

"I know," Leo said. "But Initiation is important to Tribe and us. It's the reason we still exist while others have perished."

"Plus it doesn't last long," Maria said in a soothing tone. "And when it's over, you can finally leave the compound."

Barron's nervousness quelled. "That would be great!"

"Now let's finish this delicious soup. I need to check your vitals," Maria said.

Barron lowered his spoon. "Why?"

"You have to be at your healthiest to participate in Initiation."

"I feel good," Barron said.

"Of course, you do. You're my son," Maria said. "But that's not enough for Gretchen. She needs her stupid numbers."

They finished their meal. Leo collected their bowls then carried them to the water bucket for washing. Barron was standing to leave the table when Maria waved him down.

"No you don't, young man." She lifted the test kit. "Remember?"

Barron frowned then plopped into his seat. Maria broke the seal on the kit, then opened it. Inside was a thermometer, stethoscope, blood pressure cuff and a blood sample kit. The faded instructions were tucked under the instruments. Maria unfolded them then read them. She knew them by heart, but it never hurt to read them again just in case Gretchen made any changes.

"Okay young man, let's do this," she said.

Barron passed the tests with no problem. The only variable was the blood sample analysis. She would have to wait for Gretchen for those results.

"So, am I alive?" Barron asked.

"No," Maria replied. "We'll have to kick you out of the compound to roam around with your friends."

"That's not funny," Barron said.

Maria hugged him. "After initiation you won't have to worry about that ever again."

* * *

THE FOLLOWING weeks were spent in preparation of Initiation. Teams scoured the nearby ruins and abandoned homes for items and trinkets for the ceremony. The city blacksmiths converted those objects into jewelry for the initiates and their families. None of this was necessary, but the town leaders understood how important celebration and recognition was to the survivors. Maria went to the seamstress to have Leo's initiation jacket resized for Barron, who was already bigger and broader than his father. After initiation, he would be a valuable addition to the Tribe. Maria couldn't help but smile.

The night finally arrived. A full moon lay its muted light on the compound, illuminating the celebrants as they made their way to Town Center. The moonlight was gradually usurped by the bonfire light, the blazing pile of hardwood and incense sending smoke and fragrance into the clear night sky.

Barron put on his jacket then buttoned it as Maria and Leo watched. He looked up at them both, a nervous smile on his face.

"So, I guess this is it," he said.

"It is," Maria replied.

He stood and Maria hugged him tight then kissed his forehead.

"Everything will be fine," she whispered.

Maria stepped away and watched Leo hug him.

"See you on the other side," he said.

They picked up their instruments. Maria's tambourine was weathered but still useful. Leo's shaker gourd was missing a few beads but still sang with every motion. They could hear the drumming inside their tent, so they played in syncopation.

"Lead the way, son," Maria said.

Barron danced out the tent in time with the rhythm flowing throughout the compound. Maria and Leo followed, matching their beat with the drums. They joined the other families prancing their way to Center, some with initiates, some without, but everyone joyful. As they reached the center, Maria and Leo joined the ring of parents and relatives of the initiates. Behind them stood the other Tribe members, their expressions just as joyful as the parents. New initiates meant new hope for a better future.

Standing before the fire was Gretchen. The cold expression and clinical clothing were gone, replaced by a hand-woven woolen dress that fell from her shoulders to her ankles to rest on the insteps of her bare feet. A mural decorated the garment, an abstract story of the Tribe, from its founding to the present day. As far as they knew, they were the only humans thriving in this new world. It was because of the gift bestowed on them decades ago, a protection that would now be given to their new initiates.

Standing on either side of Gretchen were her acolytes, people chosen for training so that one day they would take her place. They wore wooden masks with slits to represent their eyes and mouth. Black robes covered their bodies, and they too were shoeless. Each held a large gourd in their left hands, a small cup in their right.

The initiates walked in time with the pulsing music until they reached Gretchen and the acolytes. Maria reached out and grasped Leo's hand and they shared a smile. They watched Barron turn to his right, walking a few paces then stopping just beyond the acolyte. Once the others were in place, they swayed in time with Gretchen and the acolytes. Gretchen raised her arms; she let them drop.

The drumming ceased.

The camp fell silent.

"Tribe!" she shouted. "What are we?"

"We are one!" Maria shouted with the others.

"Tribe!" she shouted again. "What are we?"

"We are life!" they responded.

Gretchen began pacing.

"Twenty years ago, we were blessed," she said. "A man who owed us nothing gave us everything. Since that day we have prospered, able to live free of the plague that possesses others. His only demand of us was to share with others, to one day make the world free as it once was."

Gretchen turned her back to Maria and the other parents to face the new initiates.

"You have been among the Tribe since the day you were born. Tonight, you become a part of the Tribe. From this day forward you will share our responsibility upon your shoulders. But do not worry. We are here to love, nurture, and support you."

Gretchen took the large gourd from the acolyte on her right.

"Kneel," she commanded.

Maria's throat went dry. Barron knelt with the others then glanced back at her. He smiled nervously.

"Hold out your hands," Gretchen ordered.

Barron returned his attention to Gretchen, holding out his hands. The second acolyte gave each initiate a cup which Gretchen filled from her gourd. Maria grimaced as she remembered drinking that same concoction. It was nasty but necessary for what was to come. The others watched with the same remembrance, spouting encouragement to the initiates as they forced the drink down.

Gretchen waited until the final initiate finished before signaling the first acolyte. They brought her a worn leather case, the same case that once held the first vials of the lifesaving serum. The acolyte followed Gretchen to the first initiate and opened the case. Gretchen took out the needle, swabbed the initiate's arm, and administered the shot.

"Haynes!" she called out.

Doretha and Samuel Haynes hurried to the circle, catching their daughter before she collapsed. The others cheered as they led her away to their home to recover from the inoculation.

Maria barely heard the other names announced as she watched Barron waiting his turn. After what seemed like an eternity, she heard Gretchen call out their name. Leo was already on his feet and making his way to the inner circle. Maria pursued him, her face hot with emotion. They reached Barron at the same time, wrapping him up like a winter's blanket. Barron looked upon them with bleary eyes, grinning through the obvious pain.

"I did it," he whispered.

Maria kissed his cheek.

"Yes, you did. Now let's get you home."

They carried their son home amid the yells of praise and celebration, their burden easing as he regained his strength. By the time they reached their tent he was almost walking on his own.

"I'm okay," he said.

"No, you're not," Leo replied. "You just think you are."

"I feel fine," Barron argued.

"Trust us, son," Maria said. "We've done this a few times. Everybody feels they're okay until they fall flat on their face. Let's avoid that broken nose."

Barron shrugged and allowed them to take him to his cot. As they eased him down, he swooned. Maria steadied him.

"Wow. Wasn't expecting that," Barron said.

Maria grinned. "See? Let's ease you back on this cot."

Maria and Leo lowered Barron onto his thin mattress. He closed his eyes and sighed.

"This feels good."

"Keep an eye on him," Maria said to Leo. "I'm going to brew some soup."

"I'm not hungry," Barron said.

"You will be," Maria replied.

She went outside and started a fire then went to the well for water. Going back into the tent for soup bones and herbs, she saw Leo hovering over Barron. Relief washed over her as she returned to the fire with her cooking pot. Their boy was safe now, able to travel anywhere without fear. Once they were sure he was fully immune they would do what they always planned; leave the Tribe. Without the zombie threat there was no reason for them to stay.

Maria finished the soup. She filled the stone bowl then took it inside. Barron was sitting up. He smiled when he saw her and licked his lips. Maria laughed.

"Told you you'll be hungry."

She handed him the bowl and he looked at its contents and frowned.

"That's all?"

"You're not ready for solid food yet," Maria said. "But you can have all the soup you can eat."

"Yeah, it's not like it's going to stay around long," Leo said.

Barron's eyes widened. "What are you talking about?"

"You'll see."

Maria and Leo nursed Barron through the night. By morning he finally slept, and they did, too. Maria was the first to wake early that afternoon. She rummaged through their stock for a few items to trade then hurried to the central market, returning home with bread, a freshly dressed chicken and a few potatoes. Leo was cleaning the tent when she entered. Barron sat on the edge of his cot, a tired look in his eyes.

"Is it over yet?" he asked.

"You tell us," Maria said. "How do you feel?"

"Like I've been hit by a hammer," Barron said.

"You're better then," Maria said. "It will take at least three days. Your body is going through profound changes. Once it's done, you'll be like us. You'll be able to go anywhere."

"How soon?" Barron asked.

"Two weeks at the most," Maria said. "Then when you're rested, we'll take you Out."

Barron's eyes lit up. "Finally!"

"Calm down," Maria said. "Going Out is not an adventure. It's essential work. And despite your vaccination, it's still dangerous. There are other monsters to deal with."

"Other monsters?"

Barron's worried look made Maria wish she hadn't mentioned it. She patted his shoulder.

"Don't worry about that. It's nothing we can't manage.

Maria and Leo resumed their duties with each taking turns with Barron.

Twelve days after the initiation he was fully recovered and ready for his first trip Outside. Maria bartered with other villagers to get him the proper gear. Leo found him a 12-gauge shotgun in good condition, something that would keep him safe while not requiring accuracy. Though Barron had taken shooting like others in the camp, there was a huge difference between shooting targets and a real firefight.

Maria woke Barron that morning with a gentle nudge.

"Come on, villager," she whispered. "It's time."

Barron sprang up, almost bumping heads with Maria.

"Calm down!" she said. "Let's eat breakfast then head out."

They sat at the table, eating oatmeal and dried beef before getting their gear. Leo inspected Barron.

"Remember to stay close to us," he said. "Our sweep is going to take us to an area where the undead wander."

Barron's eyes went wide. "Why?"

"We need to make sure you're protected," Maria replied. "This is the only way to find out."

"But what if they're too many?"

"We're traveling with the other initiates," Leo said. "There will be enough of us to make sure nothing happens."

Leo stood back from Barron then smiled.

"You're as ready as you're ever going to be."

"Good," Maria replied. "Let's go."

They met the other families outside the town gates then proceeded on their sweep. The Haynes led the trek, their daughter walking timidly between her parents. Maria, Leo, and Barron brought up the rear.

"Why are we in the back?" Barron asked.

"It's just as important to keep an eye on where we've been as it is observing where we're going."

"Will the undead try to sneak up on us?" Barron asked.

Leo shook his head. "They're not that clever. It's the others we're concerned about. The others like us."

"Other people? Why?"

Maria draped her arm on Barron's shoulders.

"You have lived a privileged life, especially during these times. We were lucky to find Tribe, even luckier that they accepted us. They shared the Gift with us, and everything else. We have crops and livestock. What we can't make, we scavenge from the nearby towns. Others are not so fortunate. They fend for themselves, living off what they can find, or what they can take."

"Like the undead?" he asked.

"Something like that, except they live and breathe like us."

Barron looked thoughtful for a moment.

"Why don't we just share with them?"

Maria sighed. "We tried, but there's something about people in times of scarcity. Some see generosity as weakness. It's also why the founders set up our town among the undead. They can't reach us here. But we can reach them."

"Are they our enemies?"

Maria shrugged. "They're certainly not our friends."

"Initiates!"

Carla Haynes's call ended their conversation. Maria and Leo followed Barron to the others. Carla stood at the top of a steep hill. She waved everyone up. They saw the wrecked city in the valley below, a dilapidated sprawl bordering a wide river. There was movement between the structures.

"Looks like a horde," she said to Maria as she handed her the binoculars. "A good time to confirm."

Maria's hand shook as she handed the binoculars back. Carla shared a reassuring smile.

"It's just routine," she said. "You should know."

"Yeah, but he's still my son."

"And Jennette is still my daughter," Carla said. "We have to confirm."

Carla didn't wait for Maria's or any of the other parents' approval. She didn't need it.

"Initiates!"

The new citizens gathered around her.

"We're going into that town. We've spotted undead inside. You're taking the lead."

The young initiates looked at each then their parents. Maria forced a smile as she looked at Barron.

"It's okay," she said. "We'll be close behind. There's nothing to worry about."

Barron smiled and nodded. He cocked his pump action shotgun then stepped forward. Maria wondered if the confident look on his face was real or bravado. The other initiates fell in with him, their eyes on him. He was taking the leadership among them, which was good.

"Spread out," Carla said. "Make a single line and approach slowly."

The initiates did as ordered, Barron in the center. They marched toward the city, guns ready. Maria and Leo formed another line with the parents and other expedition members, keeping a few meters behind them. The closer they came to the city without incident, the better Maria felt. The undead didn't sense them. The serum injected into all of them rendered them invisible, because they emitted the same odors of the undead. Smell was the primary sense of the unfortunate dead, all other senses secondary.

Carla raised her binoculars, then jerked them down.

"Stop!" she shouted.

Maria rushed to her side. "What's wrong?"

"They're coming."

"What?"

"They're coming!"

"Everyone fall back!" Maria shouted.

"Wait," Carla said. "We must do this the right way. One of the initiates' serum didn't take. We need to know who."

"What are you saying?"

"We pull them back one by one."

"That's crazy!"

"We can't jeopardize the safety of Tribe," Carla said.

Maria wanted to protest, but she knew Carla was right. They had to know.

"Initiates!" Carla called out. "Stay where you are. Pull back beyond the second line when your name is called."

Maria took her place beside Leo while Carla called out the initiates' name. With each call, the undead continued to advance. Maria checked her rifle over and over as they came closer, her eyes fixed on Barron. The last initiates remaining were Barron and Michelle Haynes. The undead continued to come.

"Barron!" Carla shouted.

Maria watched as Barron touched Michelle's shoulder then whispered in her ear. He backed away until he was behind and beyond the second line. The undead slowed, then stopped.

"Oh God!" Maria said. She broke the line, running to Barron with Leo close behind.

"Let's go now!" she said.

Barron was dumbfounded.

"Mama, what's going on?"

"Let's go son," Leo said.

Maria grabbed Barron's arm then led him away. The trio marched nonstop back to the compound in silence, each of them caught up in their own thoughts. The guards let them enter, the curiosity evident on their faces. They didn't stop until they were inside their tent.

"Mama, what's wrong?" Barron asked.

Maria couldn't answer. She looked at Leo then dropped her face into her hands.

"Son," Leo began. "When Carla called you back to the line, the undead stopped their advance."

Barron eyes went wide. "What does that mean?"

"It means your shot didn't take," Leo replied. "See, the serum makes us invisible to the undead by incorporating part of them into us. When they sense us, they sense their own. It's how we can live here, how we thrive without fear of them. Since your serum didn't take, the undead could possibly find you here. They could find the entire compound."

Barron sat hard. "Oh."

Maria lifted her head and watched Barron's eyes dart between her and Leo.

"Will they make us leave?" he asked.

Leo began to answer, but Maria stopped him with a headshake.

"We don't know," she said. "We'll have to wait and see."

"But if I'm a threat to Tribe . . ."

"Let's just wait," Maria said.

The rest of the patrol arrived at the compound at dusk.

Maria, Leo, and Barron were eating their evening meal when Carla entered their tent. She scanned with a sympathetic gaze before speaking.

"Maria, Leo. Let's talk outside."

They followed her out of the tent.

"You saw what we all saw," Carla said. "Best you do what you need to do on your own and don't make a big scene about it. You've been here a long time, and everyone loves you, but you know how important it is that we keep Tribe pure."

"No," Maria said.

Carla sighed. "Come on, Maria. I hate this as much as you do."

"No, you don't," Maria replied. "It's not your child. I want to talk to Gretchen. I want Barron to take another shot. Maybe Gretchen got it wrong."

"She didn't," Carla replied. "He was the only initiate the undead responded to."

"I don't care. I want Gretchen to give him another shot!"

Maria pushed by Carla, striding to Gretchen's clinic. She ignored the receptionist's efforts, stomping through the narrow hall until she reached the office. Gretchen sat at her desk as if expecting her.

"I knew you would come," Gretchen said. "Carla informed me before she went to you."

"Give him another shot," Maria said.

"It won't do any good," Gretchen replied.

"How do you know?" Carla asked. "Have you done it before?"

Gretchen shifted in her chair as if she sat on a tack.

"No, but . . ."

"Then do it now," Maria said. "As much as Leo and I have done for you, we owe us that."

"It's not that simple," Gretchen replied. "It took years and lives to develop the serum. The body can tolerate one dose. Anything beyond that can cause unexpected consequences."

"Do you know this for a fact?" Maria asked.

"No, but the doctor's notes are thorough. I have no reasons to doubt him."

Maria dropped into a chair before Gretchen's desk.

"Please, Gretchen," she said. "I can't have Barron living like this, constantly fearing those things. I have to try. We have to try."

"It's not so bad," Gretchen said. "You can stay with Tribe. I'll push through a waiver. There's no reason we have to be as rigid as we were in the past. But Barron can never leave the compound again."

"I can't have him live a life like that without trying," Maria replied. "Please, Gretchen. Please."

Gretchen steepled her fingers, a distant look on her face.

"If it works, it will be a breakthrough," she said.

"It will work," Maria replied.

Gretchen finally looked at Maria.

"Get me another specimen," she said. "Something fresh."

Maria jumped to her feet. "Yes! I'll go now."

"He'll have to be quarantined in the clinic until the symptoms subside," Gretchen said.

"Of course," Maria replied.

She worked her way around the desk then wrapped Gretchen in a tight hug.

"Thank you."

Maria hurried out of the clinic. Leo and Barron jumped to their feet when she entered the tent.

"Grab your gear, Leo. We're going for a specimen."

"What about me?" Barron said.

Maria went to Barron, placing her hands on his cheeks.

"You're going to be all right. Stay in the tent and don't let anyone in until we return. Understand?

"Yes, mama."

She kissed him then left the tent. Carla met her outside.

"Where are you going?"

"Back to the city for a specimen."

"So, Gretchen agreed to try again?"

"Yes."

"I'm coming with you."

Maria stopped then spun around.

"No, you're not. A few minutes ago, you were ready to kick us out. We don't need your help."

"It wasn't personal," Carla replied. "The Tribe comes first. What you're doing might save others."

"Fuck the Tribe," Maria said. "I'm doing this for my son. If I see you following us I swear to God I'll blow your brains out."

Maria stomped away before Carla could respond. She was out the gate and crossing the protective clearing when Leo caught up with her.

"What's the plan?"

"We go back to the city, snatch an undead, get our specimen and come back."

Leo looked around. "It's dusk. We should probably wait until morning."

"Either help me or go back," Maria said.

"I'm with you, you know that," Leo said. "It's just . . ."

"It's our son, Leo! Our son!"

Leo looked away. "You're right. Let's go."

They hurried over the rough terrain, reaching the town as the last sunlight trickled below the western horizon.

"We can't go in after dark, you know that right?"

"I know," Maria said. "We'll lure them out here."

"With what?"

Maria reached into her bag then took out a large flashlight. No one in the compound knew she owned it; if they did it would be confiscated by camp enforcers. She was lucky to have discovered batteries that still held a charge, which she never used unless in emergencies. Leo looked at the light and said nothing.

Maria turned on the light. The beam illuminated a small area just outside the town outskirts.

"We're not close enough," she said.

They gathered their gear and moved closer until the light revealed the damaged building walls. Leo aimed his rifle in the direction of the light, his face tense. Maria flashed the light off and on for an hour before spotting movement.

"Something's coming," she said.

Leo raised his rifle to his shoulder. Maria let the light stream as the undead emerged from the dilapidated structures, trudging in its rambling way.

"Looks like one so far," Leo said.

"All we need," Maria replied.

They walked toward the being, closing the gap quickly. They were within killing range when Maria held up her hand. More undead stumbled from the building. Maria turned off the light.

"Can't see well," Leo said.

"Shoot where it was," Maria replied.

Leo aimed then fired. The rifle report echoed across the dark emptiness and the distant hills. Maria flashed the light; the undead lay in the grass, its body twitching in a second death. Leo took out a machete, Maria her shotgun. Leo made quick work of the carcass, chopping the arm free then wrapping it in canvas as Maria watched the other undead.

"Let's go."

They trotted away. Maria looking behind them. The other undead milled around their victim, some staring blankly at the body, others looking into the darkness. The grim scene faded as they crested the hill then descended into the expanse leading to the compound. The gate was secured; Maria pounded it until the sentries let them in.

"Go get Barron," Maria said. "I'm headed to the clinic."

Maria was sure Gretchen was asleep, but she didn't care. She banged on the door until the doctor answered. Gretchen looked disgruntled as she let Maria in, but she didn't protest. She went to the lab and prepared the instruments as Maria took out the appendage and placed it on the table.

"It will take a few hours to prepare the vaccine," Gretchen said as she worked.

"I'll wait," Maria replied.

Maria walked to the waiting room. Leo and Barron arrived a few minutes later. Barron, his eyes heavy with worry and fatigue, managed to smile before plopping onto a seat and falling back to sleep. Leo sat beside Maria.

"Get some sleep," he said. "I'll take first watch."

"I can't," she said. "Not until Barron gets the vaccine. You go ahead."

Leo settled into his chair then immediately fell to sleep. Maria watched them both, her eyes damp. She loved them both without bounds. She couldn't imagine being without either of them. Sleep slowly overwhelmed her despite her diligence.

"Maria."

Maria sat upright, looking about to find Gretchen's serious face.

"It's done. Let's get Barron prepped."

Maria stood then woke Barron. He stood without question then followed them into the office. Gretchen motioned to the chair and Barron sat and rolled up his sleeve. Gretchen administered the shot quickly.

"Same instructions as before," she said. "Take him home and

let him rest. He might have a slight fever and fatigue. When the fever breaks, bring him back."

Maria hugged Gretchen. "Thank you for doing this."

Gretchen freed herself. "Don't thank me yet. We still have to take him out again once he's recovered to make sure it took. You can thank me then."

Maria led Barron back to their tent. He lay in his bed, a hopeful smile on his face.

"It will be okay, mama," he said. "This time will take."

Maria shared a smile she didn't feel.

"I know, baby. Just rest. I'll be right here."

The days passed and Maria stayed. Barron's symptoms came, and she did what she could. Leo watched over both of them, making sure they ate and relieving Maria when she needed to rest or relieve herself. The compound took on an eerie silence despite everyone going about their routines, each person concerned about Barron's condition. But like Maria, all they could do was wait.

Seven days after the re-inoculation, Maria awoke during the night. She was thirsty, her mouth dry from sleeping with it open. She had no doubt been snoring, something Leo accused her of for years which she denied. She decided to check on Barron. He was still, his eyes wide.

"Barron?"

Maria shook him and he didn't respond.

"Barron!"

She grabbed his shoulders, staring into his blank orbs. Leo came behind her.

"What's going on?"

Maria turned to him, tearing running from her eyes.

"He's dead!"

Leo moved her aside, pressing his fingers against his neck. He jerked his hand away then grabbed Maria, pulling her back.

"He's not dead," he said.

Maria glared at him. "What do you mean he's not dead."

Leo laid his hand on her shoulders.

"We have to get him out of here. Now."

"What the fuck are you talking about? What are you . . ."

She saw the answer in Leo's eyes. Her arms dropped to her side, and she turned around.

"Oh God. Oh God no."

Barron's eyes focused on her. There was no emotion, no recognition.

"Help me," Leo said.

Maria couldn't move. She watched Leo take rope from their storage chest then use it to tie Barron's arms to his torso and secure his ankles. He went back to the chest and returned with a canvas bag that he draped over his head then tied shut.

"Help me lift him," he said.

Maria leaned for Barron but as she reached out to touch him, she found her hands frozen. She looked up into Leo's eyes.

"I . . . I can't . . . It's my . . ."

Leo touched her cheek.

"It's okay. I'll do it."

He cradled Barron into his arms then maneuvered him over his shoulder. Maria hurried to the tent flap then opened it.

"We'll need horses," he said.

"I'll get them," Maria replied.

She ran to the stables, staying as quiet as she could manage. The compound was asleep, even the guards had dozed off. She saddled two of the most docile horses then led them to the tent. Both pulled back when she neared Leo and Barron. Maria patted them as she struggled not to break down. Leo lifted Barron onto the mare then climbed onto the saddle. Maria mounted the other horse, and they rode to the gate. As they neared it, they saw a person standing in the middle of the road holding a shotgun.

"Gretchen," Maria whispered.

She ambled to them.

"You should end it here," she said.

"Get out of the way," Maria replied.

"What are you going to do?" Gretchen asked. "Set him free? To what?"

"We'll do what we have to do," Leo said. "But not here."

Gretchen nodded. She went to the gate then opened it.

"I'm sorry," she said. "I hoped it would work."

"Me, too," Maria replied.

Once they were a distance away from camp they urged the horses to a gallop, riding hard until they reached the river and the old town. Leo climbed down from his horse then lowered Barron to the ground. He untied his arms and legs then removed the bag.

"Let's go," he said.

"No," Maria replied. "Let's wait."

Together they watched for the inevitable. After an hour Barron, or what used to be Barron, sat up then struggled to his feet. He turned to them; his eyes locked on Maria.

"Give me something," she whispered. "Let me know you're still there."

But there was nothing left. Barron turned then staggered away toward the river. The tears came hard as she reached for her rifle then took aim.

"I'm so sorry," she said. "I love you. I always will."

She pulled the trigger.

The End

CECIL AND THE DISMEMBERMENT

ERRICK NUNNALLY

A*drift.*

The word popped into Cecil's head, and he couldn't deny it was the right one to describe his life. It's where he found himself this evening, unmoored from progress. Long after an embarrassing moment in a small town, a bad breakup that cost friends, and a move to another city that didn't work out. He'd pulled off a reverse hat trick. In his mind, life had become a list of things not to do. *Not* to fill your pants with hot gravy before getting on stage in school. *Not* to stay in a one-way relationship. *Not* to move halfway across the country for a half-ass, hollow opportunity. All of it led to this moment: stuck and waiting alone in a hot tunnel for a smelly rail car.

Miraculously, he was in the sweet spot between crowds and sat alone on a bench, his head leaning back against the subway tile. The feeling of the wall pressing against the back of his thick hair only reminded him that he needed a haircut—yet another expense that would cut down his already dwindling savings. The data entry job he'd fallen into only covered enough to eat and commute.

From the corner of his eye, he caught a glimpse of something reflective and didn't think anything of it. The occasional blast of hot air rattled any detritus left by commuters; it was common for foil wrappers to get spun around. He stood up and wandered to the edge of the platform, being careful not to stumble on the raised dimples of the bright-yellow safety edging. Both ends of the tunnel stretched into darkness and he could hear the screeching of wheels on rail in the distance. Nothing to indicate a train coming his way, however.

He found the train system itself fascinating. Miles of underground tracks weaving beneath the city. A mystery for commuters. What were the tunnels like when the massive trains weren't there. How would it feel to be alone inside them?

The glint caught his eye again and he spotted the eyeball near the edge of the platform. It glistened and twitched, myriad tendrils of trailing nerve and muscle contracted.

A lump pushed at the back of Cecil's throat, and he lost the sense of what to do with his hands. He stared at the gelatinous orb, and it appeared to stare back. As he crept toward it, hardly believing it to be real, it twitched again. The thing looked fresh.

This isn't possible, he thought. *Who loses an eye like this?*

He edged closer, his toe nearly touching the gore, and his phone rang. He startled like a deer and lurched backward, tipping the eyeball over the edge of the platform.

"Christ, fuck," he muttered, scrambling to pull his fliphone out. The number was unrecognized, but he answered, hoping it was a callback from one of the dozen companies he'd sent a resume to.

"Cecil!"

The voice on the other end of the line sounded urgent and familiar. Confused, Cecil said, "Who is this?"

"Did you get it?"

He couldn't imagine who would prank him like this. He'd

effectively cut ties with anyone who might've been close enough for this sort of joking.

"Who is this? Get what?"

"The eye, did you get it?"

Heart hammering in his chest, Cecil felt his mouth go dry. The train came roaring into the station, drowning out any further conversation. He stumbled onto the train, the first prickling of sweat stinging under his arm. He yelled into the phone a few more times, trying to hear over the cacophony of the train, before closing the device and shoving it in his coat pocket. He ran his hands over his knees and peered at his reflection in the windows across the train. In the fluorescent light, his normally brown skin looked pale and drawn.

The train burst into open air on the elevated track and light over the city obliterated his reflection. He could still feel the hum of panic working his jaw when he exited the train for the short walk to his run-down studio apartment.

* * *

CECIL SAT STARING at his assigned stack of documents. He cradled a mug of hot coffee, letting the steam tickle his chin. He hadn't gotten much sleep. Regardless, even on a good day, data entry crushed his soul. The phone on his desk rang.

He picked up the handset and said, "This is Cecil."

"We got disconnected last night."

Cecil's jaw clenched and he said through his teeth, "Who the fuck is this?"

"Listen, you have to go back and get the eye. It's *important*."

"Fuck you. Who is this?"

"Go back and get it."

Janice, to Cecil's right, was the first to poke her head above the cubicle wall, her eyebrows screwed into a quizzical look. Gordon, to his left, followed soon after.

Cecil hung up the phone and said, "Prank call."

His workmates traded a look and slowly sank back into their seats, resigned to fulfill the day's quota. Cecil focused on his stack of paper, trying to ignore the phone whenever it rang.

After the fourth or fifth time of Cecil ignoring calls from the unknown number, Gordon said, "Yo, Cecil, you gotta do somethin' about that, man. It's annoying AF."

"Truth," Janice said.

"Okay, okay." He picked up the phone and slammed it back down before leaving the handset off the hook. When the off-the-hook warning tone started, he slammed it back into the cradle. The unknown number rang through again, but this time he pulled the cord out of the back of the phone. At the end of the day, his supervisor called Janice in order to reach Cecil and to scold him about missing her phone calls.

* * *

It was a four-block walk to the subway. Early autumn brought with it a slight chill to the air. Cecil walked with his hands tucked into his pockets, one hand ignoring his vibrating phone. Nearly to the station, he heard a phone ringing, an old-fashioned striker on bell type. Tucked in between a liquor store and a boarded up building, bolted to the wall, the rarest of phones rang. He stopped and stared at the ancient thing, thinking it impossible. His phone had stopped ringing in his pocket and now this. He shook his head and plunged down the stairs for the platform.

The next day brought more of the same and before the intrusions could further derail his life, he decided to entertain the caller.

"What do you want?"

"For you to pick up the eye."

"Why?"

"It's important."

"It's fucking gross is what it is, man. Who is this?"

"That's not what's important, Cecil. Just get the eye. I'll call afterward."

"And you'll stop calling me?"

"Only after it's done."

Cecil sighed and hung up the phone. After spending long minutes listening to his heart pound over the clacking of keyboards around him, Janice spoke through the soft cubicle wall.

"You all right, Cecil?"

"Yeah. Yeah, I'm fine."

"Figured out how to stop that caller?"

"Yeah, maybe. I hope. Sure."

"Okay," she said. Her voice sounded as unconvinced as Cecil's thoughts.

He'd need a plastic baggie, at least, and remembered seeing some in the break room.

* * *

THE WALK to the platform took longer than usual. Cecil's every step made his legs feel like noodles—dried and fragile, or cooked and unsupportive. Either or. A small crowd of people made their way up and down the stairs. Cecil had some idea where the eye was, but getting to it would be awkward with this many people around.

'Awkward' doesn't cut it, he thought.

The entire situation was absurd. He couldn't confide in anyone; they'd think him insane. A voice on the phone?

Dismembered eye? He took deep breaths as he descended to the platform and slowly walked to the furthest end.

The train loaded and unloaded twice, while he waited, and a steady flow of people peppered the platform. It irritated him—an irrational feeling in light of the madness of the situation. Fatigued with tension, Cecil knelt at the edge of the platform and peered over, scanning the darkness beneath him.

A few travelers noticed. Cecil smiled at them and said, "Dropped my phone, can you believe it?"

He looked down the track, determined it was safe enough, and hopped down. In the darkened space between rail and wall, he spotted the eye and bent over. He removed the bag from his pocket, inverted it, and picked up the organ. It was lighter than he expected. It twitched, orbiting in his fingers. Revulsion sped up his throat. He choked it back and swapped the eye with the phone in his pocket.

Cecil stood up, held up his phone and said, "Got it!"

A few passengers rolled their eyes. He climbed back onto the platform and heaved with a small bit of relief.

AT HOME, Cecil peered at the eye in the baggie on his table. It was a brown eye, he noticed, same color as his own. It still twitched and rotated, as if looking about. He wondered at the race of the person missing an eye. Was that something that could even be determined, at this point? Could any characteristics be determined, or the eye returned? Should he call the police?

Not unless I want a beating and some jail time, he thought.

His phone rang. It was the unknown number. He swallowed, flipped open his phone, and pressed the 'speaker' button. He placed the phone on the table next to the eye and said nothing.

The familiar voice rang out. "You have it?"

Cecil worked his jaw and said, "Yeah."

A sigh of relief from the line. "Okay, good."

"Now what? This is over, right? We're done."

The sound of a dismissive huff raked Cecil's ears before the voice said, "Now you gotta find the rest down there."

Cecil sat up. "The rest of what?"

"The body."

"No." He shook his head as the first threads of panic reached his eyes.

"Stay calm, okay? All you gotta do is find the rest of the body. It'd help if you worked for them."

"Them *who*, man?" Cecil caught himself shouting and willed himself to dial it down.

"The Transportation Authority. You should get a job there. You like the trains anyway."

Cecil stood up, unable to sit any longer. "How do you know this?"

"It's not important."

"It's important to me."

"Maybe."

"'Maybe?' What *is* important to me, then, motherfucker?"

"Getting a better job, to start."

"Oh? And how do I do that?"

The voice told him how.

* * *

CECIL ACCEPTED the bundle through the iron grate and the old man on the other side said, "Welcome to the Transit Authority, kid. Sign here."

He signed and peered at the collection of hand-held equipment atop a bright orange safety vest peaked by a miner's helmet. Starting today, he was a signal trainee.

The phone calls kept coming, but they'd become more encouraging, offering advice as often as cajoling Cecil to take action. Within a few weeks, he was being sent on assignments alone in the tunnels. Cecil took to the work quickly; being in the tunnels fascinated him.

The hunt never changed, though. It was what lent an edge to every moment of his day. Go in, get the job done, and go home. The calls nagged at him, they prodded gently until he made it a habit to stay on the lookout for more body parts. He wanted to give up and simply work.

Then he found the finger.

At first he thought it was a worm because it moved. Like the eye, it twitched and beckoned, seeming to be desirous of something it could not find. Cecil pocketed the digit, suppressing the urge to vomit whenever it squirmed in his pocket. The same day, he found the rest of the hand, the other eye, and another hand, intact. The parts writhed and he shuddered with every move. Somehow the teeth were the most disturbing. They didn't move, but...teeth. At the time, he didn't realize they were an incomplete set until he found the jaw with some teeth missing.

* * *

Cecil sat on the floor between his bed and the kitchenette. He stared at the body parts writhing on the floor. When the phone rang, he didn't flinch. It was routine, an expected call nowadays.

"How many now?"

Cecil snarled, still unable to place the familiar voice. "Two hands, two eyes, two feet—one wearing a workboot—teeth, and the jaw. It's...it's just so...creepy. This is nuts."

"It's necessary. Hang in there. And good job, you're doing great."

"Am I? This was probably a transit worker like me and now

look at him: scattered all over the tunnel. Somehow still...alive? Kind of alive, I guess."

"You are doing great, man, this is a good thing, you'll see."

"Uh-huh."

As he watched the parts, a macabre thought occurred to him. He pushed the finger into the missing space on the incomplete hand. The parts slipped together.

"Holy shit!"

"What? What is it?"

"The, the, the finger it joined with the hand."

"Progress!"

"Uh, yeah, it's great. Hold on."

He started fiddling with teeth, placing them in the jaw. Each tooth, when placed correctly, sucked into place with a gentle, wet pop. It was the simplest, most disturbing puzzle.

"Are the teeth in?"

"The teeth are in."

The voice on the other line whooped and said, "You deserve a break, man. Why not go out and grab a drink?"

"By myself?"

"Yeah, why not? Just one. Can't hurt."

"I guess not. Huh. It's just..."

"What?"

"These, uhm, body parts, they're kind of...ripe."

"Then light a candle, man. You got at least one, I know."

Cecil rolled his eyes, annoyed that this person seemed to know him, and hung up the phone. He grabbed his suitcase and piled the parts in so they'd stay in one place. Then he cracked the windows to let the cool autumn air in and lit a scented candle in a bowl before leaving the apartment.

It felt good to be outside and wearing new clothes. With a haircut and the rent paid, he felt like a brand new man. A man with a job that paid a living wage. For the first time in months, 'adrift' wasn't a word that wholly defined him anymore. Or did it? This was all something new, for sure. His mind ground on the situation as he sat down in a nearby bar and ordered a beer. It was still early and uncrowded. The vibe was pleasant and as relaxing as it could be for someone with a suitcase of body parts at home.

The thoughts kept hitting him as the people scattered around the bar chatted. The patrons created a space of convivial air while Cecil maintained a vacuum around himself.

"Excuse me?"

Cecil looked to his right.

A woman with short wavy hair, a long neck, and very dark skin waved at him. "Hi. Sorry to bother you, but could you hand me a napkin?" She pointed.

In front of him and to the right lay a bartender's tray of accessories—one of which was a stack of red cocktail napkins.

"Oh, sure." Cecil dug out a few and handed them to her.

"Thanks." She used the napkins to dry a length of moisture on her forearm. "I leaned right into this puddle here," she said and smiled.

It was a nice smile.

"You're welcome," Cecil said. "It's, uh, kind o' nasty when that happens." *Not as nasty as wiggling body parts in your suitcase, Cecil.*

"Tell me about it." She wadded up the napkins and placed them on the bar. "I didn't mean to disturb you; seems like you were deep in thought."

"I guess I was, yeah. Lot of…change recently." *Like keeping body parts in your apartment, Cecil.*

"Really? Good stuff, I hope?" She winced. "I'm sorry, I don't mean to pry."

"Oh, no, well, I moved here a couple years ago and it didn't go well—" *Not as well as locating and collecting body parts, Cecil.* "—and I ended up in a lousy job, but a couple months ago, I found a gig doing work I'm interested in and things are, y'know, better." He held his hands out as if comparing the weight of one problem against another. His heart banged against his sternum, each beat a reminder every second of what he'd gotten mixed up in.

"Well, that's good. We spend too much time at work to hate it; you blessed." She arched her eyebrows and smiled. "My name's Sonya, by the way."

"Cecil." He took her offered hand.

Cecil smiled back. Her makeup matched her outfit well, he noticed, and the earrings dangling from her ears matched the pattern stitching, of all things.

"Very cool that you found earrings to match the patterns in your dress."

"Thank you for noticing!"

A woman who looked just as good as Sonya waved from across the room to get her attention.

"That's my girl, gotta go."

"Have a good night," Cecil said and nodded.

"Thanks; you too." She grinned and paused to snap a business card out. "Give me a call sometime, Cecil."

Surprised, he took the card and said, "I—thanks. I will." *You can't, Cecil.*

She hustled out, laughing with her friend, and Cecil peered at the card. It had Sonya's first name at the top and a phone number beneath it. A plain card for a not-so-plain woman. Cecil's life was hardly average nowadays. He felt that he'd somehow dodged a bullet; now was not a time for any sort of relationship. Swallowing hard, he wondered just what he was doing and at what point someone would notice that he'd gone insane.

* * *

CECIL STOOD over a pair of legs desperately in need of feet and a torso. The knees occasionally flexed, causing the pair of limbs to rock. His skin crawled, watching them in the singular beam of his headlamp. At least they were wearing pants, a well-worn pair of jeans. The legs were too large to carry easily and really wasn't this getting out of hand? He had work to do—at least two signals to clear before exiting the tunnel.

He'd done well with his supervising mentor, Mickey Struthers. The good work he'd done to date was the only reason he got to go down some tunnels on his own. Best to check those two signals and maybe get on with his life, at this point.

A half hour before quitting, Cecil checked in with Mickey.

"Here's the paperwork clearing the last three signals."

Mickey took the clipboard of papers and glanced at them. "Looks like you checked everything off okay. Got the box?"

Cecil checked his vest, feeling the device in his pocket that recorded maintenance checks.

"Ah, shit, must've left it on the last signal box. I'll go grab it, be right back."

"Sure, kid. That thing'll come outta your paycheck you don't find it!"

Cecil waved over his shoulder in response. As soon as he'd rounded the corner, he dipped into the locker room and grabbed the gym duffel he used to store a change of clothes. Emptied, it'd be just large enough for the legs.

* * *

BACK AT HIS APARTMENT, Cecil boiled a tablespoon of cinnamon. Around the small space, more candles burned. He placed a second curved plate of coffee grounds near the front door. Then he turned his attention to the remnants of the body. Since finding the legs, he'd added an arm and the torso. He squatted and stared at the torso. It wore a tattered, generic hoodie. Flecks of blood peppered the neck and shoulder. Something violent had happened to this person and here Cecil was, cleaning it up, hauling the evidence back to his apartment and—what? It wasn't even the worst part. The neck ended in tatters, countless bright red tendons and muscles twisted inside, threaded in and around the white of the spine. Bright pink and red muscles extended beyond the neck, ending in a moist tongue that twitched every few minutes.

He sank down, until he squatted, his elbows on his knees and hands in front of his mouth. He couldn't turn away.

The torso rose and fell rhythmically. It breathed at an even pace. At this level, he could see into it, the coiled organs packed in without a hint of space between them. They quivered, wet and slimy, like a cup full of swollen worms.

The phone rang. Cecil opened the device and said nothing. He couldn't take his eyes off the heaving chest.

"Tell me you got the last of it."

Cecil took a deep breath and said, "No."

"Damn. You can do this, man, you can push the whole thing forward."

He felt himself spiral. A sudden drop in his chest and he fell to pieces like this jigsaw man in front of him. Cecil slumped to the floor, his knees to his chest. The phone slipped from his hand and he sobbed, heaving on the floor. He had no idea how long he lay there, his eyes blurry, watching the torso breathe. It seemed like interminable hours, but he couldn't move, he wouldn't finish this. A briny puddle formed beneath his cheek and a chill ran the length of his body. The phone's screen remained alight and after some time, he could hear the tinny sound of his name being called over and over.

"Cecil! C'mon, please, pick up. *Please, I'll tell you who it is.*"

The raw emotion of the pleas drew his hand and he picked it up. The phone felt like a magnet on an iron floor. He struggled to drag it up to his ear. He listened to the crackle of the line and the huffs of air from his caller. "Well?"

"Okay. Okay. You are doing a good thing here, Cecil."

"Who is this, who the fuck is this? Who? Who?" Cecil surged to a sitting position and gave in to his mania, screaming into the phone.

Someone knocked on the door. He ignored it.

"Answer me."

"Get the door."

"No. Who is it?"

"You've gotta answer the door, man."

Cecil surged to his feet and screamed, "Who is it? Who is it? Who? Who? Who—"

"It's me! Okay? It's me, you're saving me."

"A name, I want a name!"

"Will you finish?"

"Answer me!"

"Will you finish?"

From the door: "Uhm, it's Sandy. We can all hear you out here. Is everything okay?"

The voice on the line repeated itself so loudly the question was distorted. "Will you finish?"

"Yes," Cecil yelled back.

"That's when you'll know. Now, answer your damn door." The line went dead.

Shit. He turned to the door and stumbled, unsure. Looking around the room, it was a sight he wouldn't want anyone to see. He put the chain on the door and cracked it.

Sandy, from across the hallway, jerked back a step. She wore a nightgown and her hair tucked under a silken cap. "What are you yelling about?"

Cecil had no idea what time it was and could tell by the way her eyes tracked that he must look terrible.

"I, uh..." He held up the phone. "I'm sorry. I was on the phone. Bad news and, uh, I didn't handle it well. I know it's late. I'm so sorry, won't happen again."

"It better not." Sandy wrinkled her nose. "What is that smell?"

"I've...been experimenting with making candles and soap. It's, um, I'll put it all away, I promise. I'm sorry."

Sandy shook her head and turned away, waving her hand in front of her nose.

Mr. and Mrs. Goreman peered through the crack of the door. Mrs. Goreman said, "Are you sure you're okay, Cecil?"

He sighed and forced a smile. "Yes, Mrs. Goreman, I'm fine. Just gotta clean up and put a few things away. All quiet from now on."

"I hope so, young man," Mr. Goreman said.

Cecil closed the door, leaned his back against it, and sank to the floor struggling not to wail.

* * *

THE NEXT FEW days were marked by a temperature drop. A literal cold as he kept all of his windows open to manage the smell. The only time he was able to get warm was at his job, in the tunnels. It made for a fine distraction, keeping his mind focused on not freezing to death rather than locating the last body part. By his account, it was the skull that was missing, everything above the lower jaw, and there was no telling if the face was in pieces too.

Cecil had been sent further down the line, beyond the commuter zone, closer to the yards. He could see the light at the end of the tunnel where trains were berthed for service. He kept telling himself that he was saving someone, doing a good thing. The deeply disturbing sight of the filthy, twitching, faceless corpse haunted his waking hours. Whenever he closed his eyes, he saw the body. And he couldn't stop wondering when he would find the final pieces and end this nightmare.

"Cecil!"

The call over the radio had the irritated urgency of someone who'd been repeating themselves.

He fumbled with his radio and answered, "Mickey, I'm here."

There was a long pause of mild static before Mickey said, "Jesus Fuckin' Christ, kid. Don't do that to me, answer your goddamn comm. Okay?"

"Right, sorry, won't happen again."

"Fuck's sake, I thought you'd gotten smushed out there or something, like, scattered on the tracks."

Mickey's wheezy, nervous laugh filled the radio.

"Still in one piece, Mick." *Unlike the corpse in your apartment, Cecil.* He swallowed hard, not quite able to resolve the tickle at the back of his throat.

"These fuckin' trains'll tear you ta pieces, young fellah, don't forget that."

"I won't."

"Okay, well, where you at on signal 224?"

"Just finished. Want me to head back?"

"Great. Yeah, I wanna clock out a bit early and you can't be wanderin' the tunnels without supervision. So finish your shift in the office. I'm sure we can find somethin' for you to do."

"Copy that. On my way."

Mickey didn't bother to respond.

In the distance, trains roared and warm air pushed through the tunnels. Cecil was grateful for the heat and the relative quiet. A long line of yellow bulbs provided just enough light to walk the line and forge deep shadows in the nooks along the way. Cecil kept his flashlight on to be safe. He was unwilling to admit that of all the things in the tunnels, it was the deep dark of the nooks that unnerved him the most. At each one, he pointed his beam of light into it. Along with the gentle crunch of his footsteps on gravel, it became a monotonous task. He almost missed the flash of yellow plastic.

Someone had lost their helmet. Probably a rail crew making repairs. Those workers dragged the most equipment around and lost plenty of it. Cecil leaned over and picked up the hard hat. Half buried in the gravel and dirt beneath it, lay most of a face and skull. He didn't flinch, had become so used to handling body parts that he figured he could be a coroner's assistant next. He'd mastered his involuntary physical reactions but the sight of such things still caused the pit of his stomach to churn with anxiety.

Squatting near the track, he eyed the find for a few moments before making a decision. His fingers buzzed as he reached to pick up the remnants of what he could only presume had been a human being at least once. His phone rang and his entire body clenched. He toppled backward onto his ass. He dug his phone out and answered through his teeth, knowing who it was.

"How the fuck—?"

"Tell me you're close. I can feel it, gimme some good news."

Cecil took several deep breaths, ignoring the caller for a moment.

"Cecil?"

"Yeah. I just…I just found the rest."

"That's great. I'll call you when you get home."

The line clicked and the caller was gone. Cecil spent one long minute staring at the half-buried face. It was filthy. And lacked eyes. The sockets were deep and unknowable. He bent to reach for the remains and hesitated, staring into the pools of black. It felt as if something would come crawling out to nip at his fingers. Instead of grabbing the skull like a bowling ball, he began pushing stone and dirt away from the back of it, exposing the top of the head. The head was covered with thick hair made of tight curls. It was interwoven with sand-like dirt and bits of stone which made it appear gray. He'd known by the skin he was collecting a Black person, but to be confronted with the final piece especially unnerved him.

He upended the crusted head, letting dirt fall from the sockets, and rolled it into the hard hat. He tucked the whole affair under his arm and hoped no one would look too closely until he could get to his locker.

When he could see the light of the platform ahead, he felt a rush of hot air at his back.

"Oh, shit..."

He'd taken too long in the tunnel, spent too much time collecting the head. A train barreled at him, its lights reflected wildly off his vest.

"Oh, shit!" Cecil ran, a piston of survival, feet pounding in the gravel. The horn sounded at his back, but he was already running as fast as possible. The roar overwhelmed his senses, and he didn't dare look back. Nothing else mattered but to get clear of the behemoth at his heels. Fear ripped at the back of his skull. It was an express, it wasn't coming in slow for pickup, it was coming in hot. Compressed air nudged him and he ran hard, straight into the station. Without pausing, he dove under the overhang of the platform. His knees scraped gravel and his chin slammed into the loose rock as he struggled to breathe. Over two-hundred tons of churning metal hurtled past, kicking up dust and debris, slamming his body with sound.

* * *

CINNAMON BOILED on the stove again and the windows were open nearly half the way up. It was the best he could do, under the circumstances. He didn't want to have another encounter with his neighbors. He couldn't stop sweating. A few scrapes bled from his chin and palms, soot and detritus caked his clothing.

The skull sat on the table and Cecil gazed into its empty eye sockets. He knew it was human, of course, but the skin sagged, lifeless, unlike the rest of the body in his apartment. The nose pulled sideways a bit and the skin was discolored beyond being recognizable as flesh.

He picked up the phone and stared at it. When it rang, he answered, "Is this an actual corpse? Did I just pick up an actual dead body part? This seems even more wrong than what we've been doing." Cecil ground his teeth together hard enough to crack. Tension rippled in his throat and his breathing came ragged and halting.

"It's the last part man, it'll be fine, you can do it."

"This is insane, I can't do this anymore..." Cecil sniffed hard, his eyes burning.

"Yes, you can, man, put me back together. Go on."

"No."

"Cecil. Do it. *Now*."

He struggled with himself before putting the phone down and carrying the head to the heaving body. His breath came in hitches as he thread the tongue through the upper jaw. Popping wet sounds floated in the air as the neck attached to the head. He picked up the lower jaw and held it in place. It snapped in like magnets were involved and the body writhed, gulping air. He took the eyes from the storage bag and dropped them into the sockets. They rotated silently and sank into place. The face rippled and flowed, skin tightening, color returning as blood rushed in and he knew.

The face, filthy and unkempt, tortured by misuse and neglect, was one he'd been seeing for years. The same one that stared back at him from any reflective surface he turned his eyes toward. It rose from the floor—*he* rose from the floor. Cecil stared at the phone, the line was still open. He snatched it and said, "Who are you? How are you doing this?"

Cecil's newly reassembled self watched, a melancholy look on his face. He held a hand out, palm up.

Cecil screamed, "Who is this? Answer me!" Gasping, he looked into his own sad, pitying eyes and asked, "Am I dead?"

His self gestured again and Cecil placed the phone in his palm.

He pocketed the phone and took a deep breath, appraising Cecil. "You're not dead, man, it's just time for you to go," he said, and placed a reassuring hand on Cecil's shoulder. "It's okay. We're going to be okay. You go ahead now." He picked up Sonya's plain card from the side table by the door. "Don't worry, I'll clean up and call her and take care of other things. You go on, we'll be fine."

Cecil trembled and sobbed, lowering his head and shaking it back and forth. When he looked up, he still stood watching, patient and encouraging.

"It was me? The whole time?" Cecil said.

"Yes. You did so good; I'll carry on. Everything will be better from now on." He held out the yellow hardhat for Cecil.

He took the helmet. Cecil nodded, rubbing the watery blur from his eyes. He left the apartment, rubbing his head and trying to think. His mind felt disconnected from everything. He floated, a lightness overcoming him, down the stairs and onto the sidewalk. He didn't remember the walk to the subway. He descended the stairs and strolled the length of the platform to the maintenance ladder and climbed down. He put on the hardhat.

No one noticed.

No one said anything.

He wore the uniform of a transit worker, after all.

Cecil walked down the tunnel until he disappeared into the shadows.

The End

GRAYED OUT

CRAIG L. GIDNEY

It took Berniece trips to three different stores to find Sour Patch Kids. CVS didn't have it, and neither did Safeway. A last-ditch effort, at Sonya's Market, she found boxes of it next to old candy bars and overpriced trail mix. It was an exceptionally ugly package, neon orange and red, and the candies looked like grayish kids with Bart Simpson hair, circles for eyes and awful grins for mouths. She couldn't imagine what they tasted like. It was probably like a cascade of artificial chemicals that had no basis in nature. Of course, the candy she'd eaten when she was young was no better. She remembered SweetTarts —sour sweet tablets and Sugardaddies, a molasses flavored candy that could rip your fillings out. It was all trash. But kids loved it. And she loved the kids that visited her apartment. She was known as the Candy Lady. They didn't know her name, and that was fine. She didn't charge much for the treats. It was a rough neighborhood, and Berniece was more than happy to be a sanctuary.

Things were getting bad these days. More violent crime, and more drugs with even stranger names. There was Tranq, Scooby

Doo, and Flakka—endlessly remixed versions of synthetic weed and fentanyl cut with cheaper and deadlier additives. Berniece remembered the days of PCP and crack, when you saw people turn into crazed juggernauts with endless rage and superhuman strength. Her ex-husband became a violent, paranoid person—once, she saw him punch a soda machine repeatedly, until his hands were bloody and full of glass shards. Years later, her girlfriend Carlie became addicted after she'd lost her job. Those drugs, as terrible as they were, she could understand. She understood fentanyl and Vicodin—they were opiates. But the new drug, sometimes called Gray—that, she couldn't wrap her head around.

Berniece took the 84 back to the Towers, her rollator basket full of candy. Ernestine was the bus driver. Her usually sour face brightened when she saw Berniece, and she didn't start driving until Berniece was settled into her seat.

"You got my candy, Miss Berniece?"

"You as bad as them kids," she replied. "I might have some Mike and Ikes...."

"You know my weakness," Ernestine laughed. "But I'll pass. I started this weight loss program. It's an app on the phone where I enter everything I eat, and it lets me know if I hit my goal."

"Any luck with that? I can barely make a phone call with these high-tech things."

"I lost a pound. But, damn, I want to eat something good once in a while. Protein and vegetables, day in and day out. No carbs, no fruit. Nothing sweet."

"Carlie tried that no-carb thing for a whole week. She was so grouchy that I made some biscuits one night. Homemade ones, with butter and crunchy tops. She couldn't resist them...."

"Miss Berniece, say it ain't so."

"Well, I couldn't stand her attitude. Besides, I believe that you can have everything—in moderation."

"I know that's right. You're in good health."

"I don't know about that. I have the Sugars, and old Arthur is in my knees. But I take medicine and watch what I eat. I just don't obsess over it."

The 84 turned a corner, and paused at a bus stop. The man who got in radiated dark energy. There were holes in his clothing—his filthy jeans, his t-shirt with the faded decal of Bugs Bunny and the Tasmanian Devil dressed in sagging jeans and Timberland boots. There were holes in the man's shoe. The man's fingernails were long and dirty, his brown skin was covered in gray—little particles of dead skin. It was a shame—he was a good-looking man. He shambled up the bus steps and jerkily made his way down the aisle. Berniece caught a whiff of him—unwashed skin, and a weird, candy-sweet smell. The whites of his eyes were yellow, like butterscotch, and they saw nothing. Ernestine and her exchanged a look. She let the Gray-addict in and didn't ask him to pay his fare.

Gray-addicts could be erratic, and one of the side effects of the drug was that they bit things. They bit the air, their skin, and sometimes, other people. She watched as his teeth chattered. His terrible teeth, yellow and crusted with food. She could only imagine what his breath smelled like. One of the other passengers got up and moved away from the man. Was he speaking? Berniece couldn't tell.

Ernestine concentrated on her route. Berniece could tell she was bothered by the Gray man. But what could she do? Anything could set them off. She heard stories of them biting people, and that their saliva was full of whatever demonic chemical flowed through the veins. The bitten would get sick, at least temporarily. Some of the bitten went on to become addicts themselves. The high was, apparently, very powerful.

The Gray man finally rang the bus bell, an admirable feat since he seemed to be whacked out of his mind. He stumble-staggered to the front of the bus and stood waiting for the stop. She heard him mutter something under his breath. At first, Berniece thought it was nonsense. It was a rhythmic whisper, and she could half-hear some sounds.

Sugar.... Glucose.... Caramel.... Syrup.... Sweet.... Sour....

The sound was barely there. The words curled, like italics.

Strawberry.... Watermelon.... Peach... Lemon....

Was Ernestine hearing this? If she was, she was ignoring it. Besides, Berniece couldn't one-hundred percent attest that the addict actually *was* speaking.

She thought, *Can he smell the candy in my rollator?*

She found herself opening up the walker's bench and taking out a bag of Sour Patch kids. They were grape-flavored. A purple gremlin-child danced on the label amid splashes of color.

The Gray addict turned his grayish face in her direction. In a way, he looked like the candy mascot—his hair was similarly spiked. Against her better judgment , Berniece tossed him the bag of candy. He caught it and smiled at her with his dead yellow teeth. Teeth somewhere between the color of old dandelions and mustard. It was a human look on a hollowed out face. She'd seen it before, on Callum's face, on Carlie's face, after they emerged from the grip of drugs. It was a look that said, *I'm a person after all.*

The bus screeched to a halt, and the door opened. The Gray man left, candy packet in hand, and lurched down the stairs.

"Why did you do that?" Ernestine asked as soon as the bus pulled away.

Berniece opened her mouth. She found that she had nothing to say. "I don't know," she finally said. "I guess he looked like someone I knew once. Someone from church."

"Girl, you know how dangerous those folks on Gray can be? Transit told us to ignore them. Just let 'em on the bus, no questions asked. There's been too many violent incidents."

"I know, it was stupid. It's just.... Nevermind."

Nevermind meant that she'd lived through several drug epidemics. Seen kids from the school where she worked turn into monsters. *Nevermind* meant that she was just so, so tired. *Nevermind* meant that she didn't want to think about it, any of it. Of families torn apart, and the deaths.

Berniece got off at the next stop. "Have a blessed day," she told Ernestine as she carefully left the bus. Her rollator was suddenly very heavy. She had to pass the foam playground, with its colorful Jungle Gym and swing sets. It was empty. It was still light out, and some of the kids from the Azalea Towers should have been out, whooping and hollering as they played. She checked her watch. School was out by now, just before evening homework and dinner. Usually, she'd be mobbed by the little ones as they clamored for candy. It was odd, but not unprecedented. She wheeled down the path, past the dormant azalea bushes that lined her building and entered the lobby.

The lobby was full. Full of children and their mamas. Some of the kids were crying, their mamas comforting them with hugs and head pats.

Berniece scanned the crowd for a familiar face, and settled on Kelondra Robins, who held her four-year old daughter Keleisha's face pressed against the front of her denim dress.

"Hey, hey," she said to Kelondra, "What happened?"

"One of those addicts came into the playground," she said, stroking her daughter's head. Berniece could see that Kelondra was shaken up. She spoke in hushed, soothing tones.

"One of them fucking Gray boys," said Demetria LeRoy. "Came wanderin' into the playground, talking nonsense. Scared the kids half to death."

"Shhh," said Kelondra. "Watch your language, Dee."

"I'm sorry. But they make me so mad. Seeing them walking

like they're half dead everywhere. I saw one the other day taking a shit down in the alley, next to the dumpsters—"

"Dee! Language. These are kids!"

Demetria's raised voice startled the children and set off a fresh wave of whimpers and cries in the linoleum tomb of the lobby. Demetria's expression was somewhere between mortified embarrassment and righteous indignation. Her lips compressed into a thin, angry line.

Rannell Johnston held her son Jaden in her arms. Jaden shivered like a leaf. She said, in a whisper, "We're freaked out cause the Gray dude bit Phaedra's kid. We had to call an ambulance. Of course, it took forever to get here."

"No!" Berniece. "Not Booker." Booker was the sweetest little boy, with his wide dark eyes and infectious bark of a laugh. He could have been on television. He was the one who wanted Sour Patch Kids.

Just as a wave of despair washed over her, she suddenly knew what to do. At least for now. She was, after all, The Candy Lady.

"Kids! I have all of your favorite candies. You can have them for free. This one time!"

The whimpering and snuffling cries stopped. Candy was the magic word. The kids detached themselves from their mamas and gathered around Berniece's rollator. The seat and basket was a vinyl treasure chest. She opened it, and handed out chocolate bars, fruit chews and other brightly colored confections like the witch in that old story.

Words echoed in her head, in that weird whisper.

Sugar.... Glucose.... Caramel.... Syrup.... Sweet.... Sour....

And the despair returned. The witch in that story ate children. What did *her* teeth look like? Were they yellowed tombstones? Was the witch gaunt and ashen?

She tried to put the thought out of her mind. (*Strawberry.... Watermelon.... Peach... Lemon....*)

She handed out candy to eager hands. She thought, *Witches aren't real. But Grays are....*

* * *

THE NEXT MORNING, Berniece took a ride-share to the hospital with Phaedra Andrews. They'd kept Booker overnight for observation, and the hospital had practically kicked her out of Booker's room, claiming that they had no room, they were stuffed to capacity. So Phaedra had gone back to Azalea Towers that evening without her son. She'd gotten no sleep. Her face was tight, and her skin had lost its luster. Berniece could see the dark circles beneath her eyes. Her hair was hidden in her night bonnet, and she wore no make-up. Usually, Phaedra was dressed to the nines, her foundation and powder immaculate. She drenched herself in perfume. Now, she was small and tired, and a stale smell emanated from her.

Berniece thought, *She hasn't even brushed her teeth.*

"I won't forget the face of the motherfucker who bit Booker," Phaedra said as she got ready. "Who the hell bites a child?"

"What did he look like?"

"He was a skinny dude, with jeans hanging off his ass. He had no ass. Just bones. His skin was so dry and ashy, it looked like he took a dust bath. The whites of his eyes were yellow, like he had hepatitis. And he wore a black hoodie with that Boondocks character on it."

"How did it happen?"

"It happened so fast. One moment, Booker was on the slides and the next, this jittering fool comes in with his Frankenstein walk and is in the play area. We tried to shoo him away. But he kept chomping at the air....

"I got up off the bench when I saw him heading to the jungle gym. But he reached Booker first...."

Phaedra paused, collected herself. "Booker screamed. He bit him on the arm. I rushed over to him. The bite was terrible. His arm looked like chopped liver, all chewed up and gray. And the space around the bite began to turn gray....

"I don't really know what happened with the creep after that. I went into crisis mode. I heard Demetria pepper-sprayed him. And that he still came after kids...."

Berniece could see the scene in front of her. The chaos, the screams. The blood. The gray man with yellow teeth and eyes. She remembered the kid from the bus, felt shame for the flicker of kindness she had shown him.

Phaedra threw on a housecoat and a pair of Crocs. At least they matched; both were bright pink. They left her apartment—reception was spotty—and Phaedra summoned the ride-share in front of the Towers.

It took the ride-share app a few minutes to pick a driver.

"The damned app keeps dropping drivers. Guess AZ Towers is too 'hood' for them!" Phaedra said.

Berniece said nothing. Instead, she rubbed Phaedra's shoulders. The muscles were tensed, as hard as stone.

"If I find that motherfucker that bit Booker, I will, *sohelpmeGod,* bash his brains in."

Berniece flinched—Phaedra was usually so poised and professional. She worked as a receptionist at a downtown law firm. Some of the other folks thought she put on airs, that she was "sadity ".

"Damnit! Another driver dropped us. I could get there faster if I walked to General..."

"Try not to focus on this small stuff," Berniece said. "Focus on Booker. He needs you."

"I know, Miss Berniece. It's just so hard. You try to give your kid the best life you can. And then something like this happens."

She glanced at her phone again. "It says that Mohamed is two minutes away.

As they walked to the pickup spot, they saw one of the Gray addicts on the other side of the street. It was a woman this time. Maybe she had once been pretty. She was a small thing, couldn't have been more than five feet, if that. She was skinny and the state of her skin, hair, and clothes made it impossible to place her age. She could have been anywhere from fifteen to her mid-forties. She wore a once-white crop-top with some indecipherable word stretched across it; the glitter of the word had flaked off. She had dusky rose pink faded jeans and sandals which displayed the crusted ruin of her feet. The Gray-girl bit the air, probably speaking a word-salad litany that no one could hear. Phaedra didn't notice the woman, or at least, ignored her. That was for the best.

A boxy blue car was waiting for them at the corner. The driver was a twenty-five-year-old man with glasses that made him look scholarly.

"About damn time you showed up," Phaedra said as she sat in the car.

"Phaedra! It's not his fault that other drivers canceled on us. Please forgive her, Mr...."

"Mohamed," said the driver, his accented voice flavored with sullenness.

"She's been under a lot of stress. Her kid's in the hospital."

Without further words, Mohamed pulled off.

"Sorry," said Phaedra, so softly that it was questionable whether the driver heard the apology or not. They rode the boulevard, flanked on all sides by blight. Past liquor stores with cardboard on their windows and vape shops that had flickering neon signs. The old grocery store was closed, the nearest one mile away. Berniece saw burnt shells of foreclosed houses, homes where her long-gone friends had lived. Underneath a train trestle were a couple of tents where Grays stumbled around with glassy eyes that saw something that wasn't there. You could tell by their mumbling, chapped lips and staccato bites at invisible things.

Phaedra looked up from her phone, looking at the wandering, lost people. "I don't see a single white person when they talk about that gray shit. Not on newscasts, not on the streets."

"It ain't no 'Opioid Epidemic', that's for sure," Berniece replied. "There's no '60 Minutes' profiles about devastated families."

"The people at my law firm call this area 'Zombie Town'. One of the attorney's clients was charged with biting a bunch of police officers. The police attorneys are trying to throw the book at him. The officers all got infections and claimed they saw hallucinations. Still saw them, months afterward."

The traffic crawled as they watched the procession of broken men and women meander down sidewalks and bumble into the streets. They were all ages. Berniece saw a woman her age—at least over 65—swat at some unseen phantasm, her mouth constantly moving. The woman wore a blue skirt patterned with bright red strawberries. Berniece had an identical skirt somewhere buried in her closet. She looked away.

Fifteen minutes later they arrived at General Hospital. She hated this hospital. It was so old. It hadn't been updated in decades. Yellow cinder block, mint-green linoleum, and long echoing halls. They signed in and got wristbands. When they got off the elevator, Berniece told Phaedra to go to Booker and not worry about her slowing her down. She'd be right behind. Phaedra took off and Berniece hobbled behind, slowly passing by a nurses' station and some kind of bulky industrial cleaning robot. She passed by patient rooms filled with sick people.

Whispering and chattering-their-teeth sick people.

She heard:

Lists of colors: *red...blue...green...pink...puce... purple... mauve... magenta.....* A spectrum of color, of Pantone hues, *mustard-yellow... navy-blue... honeysuckle... tiger lily....*

Lists of medicine: *thorazine...mirtazapine... sertraline... saline... alprazolam... escitalopram... Glucophage... trazodone....*

Lists of smells: *ammonia... vinegar... sweat... urine... acid... air freshener....*

There was a poetry to the recitation. When her Aunt Florine got the Spirit, she spoke random nonsense. It reminded her of that. Both terrifying and beautiful. Florine claimed that she was speaking the language of the angels. Surely, that wasn't the language of winged supermodels. It was the language of those Biblical angels, the ones that were collages of eyes and wings.

Lists that repeated themselves over and over, punctuated by teeth clacking. It wasn't the language of angels, though. The words were earthly and mundane. It was definitely unearthly, this breakdown into granular categorization.

Berniece thought: *This whole ward is filled with addicts.*

She walked as quickly as she could, her cane rhythmically tapping off the floor. She finally reached the room where Booker was.

Phaedra was just outside, talking to a white doctor. He, and in fact all the medical professionals, wore some kind of protective gear. Work gloves and face shields.

"But I can't afford that," Phaedra was telling the doctor.

"We can't send him home yet," the doctor said. He looked even more cold and distant with a plastic shield in front of his face. "It's a public health hazard. If he bites you, then *you* could get the infection, too. It's only a couple more days. We'll make sure that your boy is as comfortable as possible. In fact, he'll be asleep the entire time, while the drug clears his system."

"Can't you give me some sleeping medicine, and send him home?"

"We're also feeding him intravenously. Something you can't do at home."

Phaedra cursed and dipped into the room.

"I'm Booker's grandmother," Berniece lied to the doctor, whose name plate said Dr. Updike. "How long is he gonna to be out for?"

"Three days," he replied. "It takes 72 hours after the bite."

"How about the Gray—the addicts themselves? How long does it take for them to get clean?"

Dr. Updike said, "Gray is an odd cross between a steroid and a hallucinogen. We're still learning about it. If you'll excuse me, ma'am...."

He left her. Berniece went into the hospital room. Phaedra was bent over her son, who looked like he was in a deep sleep. His skin had an ashy cast to it, no doubt dried out by that horrible drug. His eyes moved restless behind his closed lids. What did he see?

"I *was* going to buy a car," Phaedra said. She didn't look up. "I wouldn't have to take two buses to get to work anymore. But this. This is going to wipe the fund out."

Berniece opened her mouth, then closed it. She was going to say some cliche thing about "at least your son will be okay," but thought better of it. Phaedra was entitled to her messy feelings. *She probably feels anger, fear, resentment, isolation, and sadness.* Identifying and listing the emotions was strangely satisfying to Berniece. The words fell like the petals of a multicolored flower. Lipstick-red anger, dandelion-yellow fear, waveringly magenta resentment, and ice-blue isolation.

"I'll grab something from the cafeteria," she told Phaedra, who said nothing.

* * *

SHE BOUGHT an overpriced coffee and muffin for Phaedra, who ignored the food, watching her sleeping son for any possible change. Every now and then, Booker would open his mouth and then quickly close it. He was four years old, his vocabulary was limited, so Berniece didn't think he would be whispering lists of random words. She said her goodbye. Phaedra offered to pay for a ride share back to Azalea Towers, which she declined. Berniece didn't quite trust those services, and besides, the 86 dropped her only 2 blocks away. She could use the walk, even with the cane.

The 86's route was also through Zombie Town. She watched as the mumbling addicts moved through the streets in staggering lurches. She watched a young woman in tattered jeans and hoop earrings bite another woman wearing a lace mantilla in front of a pawnshop. She saw a group of white kids on the opposite side of the street filming the Gray-addicts, probably for one of their YouTube videos. At least one of them was laughing.

She turned away and took out her phone to distract herself from the horrors outside her window. She opened a game of Bejeweled.

She crushed sapphires, rubies, diamonds, emeralds and....

She stopped playing the game.

Those lists. Words, images, and sounds were somehow very important to users of Gray.

It soothed them, somehow. Like candy soothed children.

She was thinking this when she got off the 86. It let her off on the back side of the AZT. Old Arthur started acting up, each step more painful than the last. Damned knee! She had to stop at the alley entrance, where the dumpsters were.

She wasn't alone. She saw someone behind the dumpster. A puff of gray smoke rose up. It smelled of death and burned candy.

"Who's there?" Berniece called out, against her better judgment. Both Phaedra and Ernestine would have looked at her like she was crazy. Maybe she was crazy, at least a little.

Whoever was behind the dumpster said nothing. She should have left it alone. Gone back to her apartment and shut her door. Locked the world outside, until someone higher up did something about it. But she knew nothing would happen, at least until it began affecting richer, whiter communities. She'd lived through it all.

"I said, who's there. Show yourself!"

Berniece was doing this for the children in Azalea Towers. For Booker. She had to know.

The person behind the dumpster finally stood up. It was a young man in a Boondocks hoodie. She didn't know the name of the mean-faced child, but she recognized the character. The man was covered in gray dust, his skin so dry it was molting. He looked at her, and his teeth began to chatter. As if he wanted to bite something.

Berniece steeled herself. Her stomach was in knots, a roiling, reeling sea. The Gray man began making his way down the alley, lurching past abandoned sofas and mattresses. He would bite her, and then she would be infected. She would become like that old woman she'd seen beneath the overpass, Grayed-out and limping, tasting and biting and muttering random lists of things.

He was getting closer. And closer.

"Orchids," she said, soft as a whisper. "*Roses. Carnations. Tulips.*"

The Gray man stopped his approach. He blinked, as if confused.

"*Violets. Daisies....*" She continued. She was worried that she would reach the end of the list. And then what? What if it didn't work? She was such a fool. Both her ex-husband Callum and her ex-girlfriend had said so.

"You're too nice," they said at separate times.

The Gray-addict stopped. He stood within arm's reach of her. He began speaking in that hypnotic whisper, that curled like italics. A calligraphic list of flowers. "*...daffodils, lilies, snapdragons....*"

His eyes drooped, not quite closed. She could see the jaundice-yellow and the dark half-moons of his pupils.

She thought, *It works! The list of things make them calm.*

His teeth had stopped chattering as he breathed further flowers into the air: *chrysanthemums....poppies.....phlox...*

While he was bewitched, Berniece lifted her cane, and hit him as hard as she could. She almost fell herself. Her knee flared with pain.

The Gray-addict fell backwards, hitting his head on the cement.

When she gained her composure, Berniece walked to the front entrance of her building. She passed a couple of loitering addicts. A woman in an overcoat headed straight towards Berniece, who did the same whispering trick. It worked on the Gray woman. The other addict, a young man, picked up the woman's rhythmic murmur until they, too, were in a trance.

The Candy Lady hobbled into the Towers, not really feeling pain. Adrenaline spiked in her brain, and she was high on revenge.

Maybe I can save them.

THE RECKONING

BRANDON MASSEY

October 1847
Richmond, Virginia

Benjamin Parker was closing his office and preparing to go home when a visitor knocked on the door.

Frowning, he set down his stovepipe hat. He rarely had visitors, and never welcomed unexpected solicitors. Had he forgotten an appointment? Although Parker Press was only a small publishing company, one of many enterprises on Broad Street, the business required managing a plethora of details; and as he approached forty years of age, forgetting some of those details had become a more common occurrence.

He opened the door. The visitor was decidedly someone with whom Benjamin would *not* have scheduled an appointment: a male Negro.

Benjamin's chest tightened, straining the buttons on his frock coat.

Benjamin had published abolitionist pamphlets about the horrors of slavery, the injustice of the practice, the need for its eradication to create a civilized society. Such views were a trend amongst his Freemason friends and business colleagues, and he didn't wish to be on the wrong side of history.

But he had never welcomed a Negro into his office or residence as anything other than a servant—and he wasn't entirely sure he wanted to, then. Writing about the civil liberties of the Negro was an academic exercise, but to welcome such a person into your place of business, or your home, as an equal, was another, more personal, matter.

The Negro looked like a runaway slave. He wore a long, heavy, gray wool coat—far too heavy for the mild weather they were experiencing—a grubby black cap pulled low over his head, tattered trousers, and muddy boots. A blue kerchief concealed much of his face, but the chestnut brown skin peeked through in small sections. He wore the mismatched clothing of a man on the run, the garments likely stolen from his master and soiled during his escape.

The Negro smelled, too. He reeked of raw earth and the wilderness and the creatures that roamed the dark places. The pungency roiled Benjamin's stomach.

A deep shade of crimson outlined the Negro's furtive eyes. Benjamin was no physician, but the man looked unwell, as if he'd not slept in weeks.

It was difficult to determine his age, but the broad span of his shoulders and his upright posture suggested a younger man.

Benjamin cleared his throat, barely trusting himself to speak. "Yes?"

Gaze darting back and forth, the Negro peeled the kerchief away, exposing his mouth and throat. His dark lips were cracked, and Benjamin saw a nasty wound encircling the man's neck, like a rope burn.

"My name is Solomon Brown, sir." He spoke in a gravelly baritone, yet had the most perfect enunciation Benjamin had ever heard from anyone. Despite this, speaking seemed to demand an effort from him; he paused, drawing in breath. "May I have a moment of your time, Mr. Parker? I wish to discuss a business matter."

What sort of business might a Negro wish to discuss with him, a reputable publisher?

But in the face of such unexpected eloquence, Benjamin didn't trust himself to reply without his childhood stutter resurfacing, and he didn't dare allow himself to stutter in front of a Negro.

He cast a look about to ensure no one saw them, then, satisfied, he nodded, and Solomon Brown entered his office.

* * *

BENJAMIN DREW the curtains on the office windows. He could not risk an accusation of harboring a fugitive slave.

Solomon Brown removed an item from the depths of his voluminous coat and placed it on Benjamin's oak desk. The thick, squarish thing was wrapped in tattered brown paper and twine.

"Ah." Benjamin tilted his head. "You have a manuscript?"

Although his company was small, he still received his share of unsolicited submissions, most of them beyond unpublishable.

"Yes, Mr. Parker." Solomon stood in front of a chair, but he didn't sink into it, and Benjamin had the impression that this Negro would do only what a white man gave him permission to do.

Later, he would discover the error of that impression.

Settling into his own chair, Benjamin peeled open the package and adjusted his spectacles. It was written in elegant handwriting—better than Benjamin's own learned script. Surely, this Negro hadn't composed it. Benjamin thought slave owners forbid the slaves from reading or writing lest they learn to rebel against their masters.

The title page stated:

A Narrative of Some Remarkable Events in the Life of Solomon Brown
Written by Himself

"A slave narrative?" Benjamin asked. It wasn't a question, but Solomon responded.

"I used to be a slave, Mr. Parker. I'm a free man."

"Is that true?" Considering this man's appearance, Benjamin found that assertion dubious. "Do you have your papers of manumission?"

Solomon's gaze slid away from Benjamin. Benjamin pursed his lips. So, he *was* a runaway slave.

"I'd like you to read it," Solomon said. "If it's to your liking, I request for you to publish it."

Benjamin pursed his lips. Slave narratives had substantial commercial appeal, did they not? That articulate Negro, Frederick Douglass, had made quite a splash with his publication two years ago. Such a project could put Benjamin's company on a proper, profitable path, and his wife, Emma, might at last realize that this business was not an expensive indulgence funded by his family inheritance. It could serve as a legitimate instrument to lift them to the lofty social heights they deserved.

Benjamin thumbed through the stacked pages. The narrative was numbered, too. It was ten chapters and twenty-seven pages. He murmured with satisfaction, already tabulating how this material might translate to a printed product, what his printer would charge for binding, and what might be a profitable price he could assign to the published book.

In retrospect, he should have asked more questions of this Solomon Brown. Such as: why are you bringing this to me? Why do I suspect you are not the emancipated Negro you claim to be? Who might be looking for you?

But Benjamin only licked his lips, literally salivating at the prospect of having a potential bestseller on his hands. Good fortune had dropped onto his desk. He could not squander this opportunity.

"I'll review it," Benjamin said. "Return to my office in seven days and I'll render my decision. Is that amenable to you?"

Solomon's eyes narrowed, and Benjamin saw something in the man's gaze that made coldness lick the base of his spine. But then it was gone, like a fleeting shadow.

"Can you finish it in three days?" Solomon asked. He glanced toward the windows, where dusk had settled over the town. "I'm bound to depart this city soon."

Benjamin tutted. "I'll have to shift aside some matters, but yes, three days it is, then. I hope it's worthy of this imposition you've presented."

At that, Solomon smiled, showing teeth that were startling in their blackness, as if this man feasted on graveyard mud.

"Every word I've written is true. Every word."

* * *

BENJAMIN and his family lived on three acres of pristine land in a prized section of town, a property that his family had held for two generations. Dense woodlands encircled the spacious residence. Deer and even wolves wandered out of that primeval forest from time to time.

As Benjamin entered his oak-paneled study that evening, he found their newly acquired maidservant dusting off his mantle. The young Negro woman flinched at his unexpected entrance.

He dismissed her with a wave, and she departed as silently as a spirit.

He eased into his rocking chair with his white clay pipe and cup of hot tea. Solomon's manuscript piled on the table beside him, the pages illuminated by the pale glow of a whale oil lantern.

His wife, Emma, came inside. She was dressed for bed in a flowing lace nightgown.

"Ah, what do you have there, Benny?" Emma asked. "Is it something interesting?"

"Wouldn't you like to know, dear?" Benjamin smiled. He didn't intend to share their likely good fortune until he was certain of the worth of the Negro's narrative. "Ask me in three evenings and perhaps I'll share it with you."

"I'm rather curious now." Her turquoise eyes twinkled. Since they had brought on the maidservant, his wife was often in fine spirits. "May I read it?"

"Soon, my dear. Now, I'll be up reading for a while. Don't wait up for me."

She pressed her warm lips against his forehead. As she leaned close, the silver necklace he had given Emma for her birthday brushed across his cheeks.

"Don't stay up too late, darling," she said, ruffling his scant hair.

With Emma out of the study, Benjamin began to read.

* * *

My name is Solomon Brown. Before I begin my narrative, I wish to share with the reader: every word written is true.

Now I shall begin.

I will always remember the day that our master took away Mary. It was near my birthday—like most slaves, I don't know the date of my birth, but according to my beloved and long-lost mother, I was born in the depths of the harvest season. Early that morning, Mary and I were out in the tobacco fields harvesting the crop when I heard hooves striking the earth, and I looked up and spied horses approaching. The white men that you never wanted to see rode upon them: our master, the overseer, and his two ruddy-faced minions.

"Good morning, y'all," Master said.

The master was about the same age as I, and I had fond memories of the time when he and I were children. It had been rumored that the master and I shared the same father. As a boy, the master had taught me to read and write and shared his storybooks with me. Since I was a child, a paralyzing stutter had afflicted me, and I believe the young master had felt pity.

But when Master's father died and he assumed ownership of the plantation, his heart hardened, as if he were ashamed of how he had once befriended a slave child, whether or not we shared the same father.

"Good morning, Master," Mary and I said. I got those words out quickly, without a stammer. Silence would have brought a reprimand.

Yet Mary's hand slipped into mine and squeezed, and I could feel the coldness in her palm.

"Come along with me, Mary," Master said. "Say your goodbyes and come on."

I couldn't believe it, but I knew it was happening. I had seen my brother ripped away from us when he was in his youthful prime and would have brought a hefty price at auction.

Mary was in her prime, too, younger than I, ready to bear children, a diligent worker with a sweet smile and lovely eyes. She had spent time working in the master's house but had been moved into field labor because I heard that Master faced a shortage of slave hands to cultivate the crops.

Mary and I had been married a season, but the white men didn't recognize our marriage ceremonies unless they performed them, which they never did. We lived in separate quarters and the only time we enjoyed each other's company was while working, or during rare times off in the evenings when we could sneak away from the others.

"M-m-m-master, I beg . . . beg y-y-you," I said, and hated how at my time of crisis I couldn't get the words to flow that I heard so lucidly in my mind. "M-m-m-Mary and I . . . must . . must be . . . together. We w-w-w-work better . . . t-t-t-t-together."

Mary nodded eagerly.

Master's smile was cherubic, but it made my heart cold.

"You work better together, is that what you say, boy?" he asked. "Then do you have six hundred dollars to keep her? That's the price for a young Negro maidservant in town."

"I c-c-c-can . . . w-w-work for it . . . Master."

At this, the white men chortled. Mary and I looked at each other.

It's gonna be all right, Solomon, she whispered. *We gonna see each other again.*

"Come along now, Mary," Master said, with a nod.

Mary hesitated, then stepped forward, but I did not release her hand.

"P-p-p-p-please . . . Master."

"You release her hand, boy, or I'll deliver you a whipping you won't soon forget."

"Solomon, please . . ." But Mary didn't let go, tears falling down her cheeks.

Master snarled like a beast, and the overseer brought down the leather whip on me, lashing my arm. It felt like fire on my flesh. I spun away and fell to the ground.

As I lay in the warm dirt, they took away my Mary, my wife, my life.

I'll get back to you, I promised, watching the horses recede in a cloud of dust. *I will find you and we will be free.*

* * *

NOT LONG AFTER they took away my Mary, I planned to run away to find her.

I had heard from one of the house slaves that Master had sold Mary in Richmond and was pleased with the price she had brought, crowing to his wife about his business sense. I would need to get to Richmond to have any hope of locating her.

"You be a fool, niggah," Blind Man Robert said. We were in our assigned cabin one evening after we had finished our work. Blind Man Robert was the oldest Negro on the plantation but still labored in the fields, his back battered by so many years of grueling work that he couldn't stand straight. He used a thick knobby stick to help him feel his way around. Although blind, or nearly so, he worked mostly every day like the rest of us.

His dark, sour face wrinkled like old boots. "Forget 'bout that gal, you hear? She be gone now. All you gonna do is earn yourself another whippin'."

"W-w-w-where is Richmond?" I asked him. Although ill-tempered and sightless, he had vast knowledge of the surrounding lands.

Blind Man Robert spat out a wad of something foul and oily.

"Three days' North," he said. "So, I hear it be said. You ain't never gonna get that far 'fore Master gets his hounds on you."

I suspected that Robert had once tried to escape on his own, back when he had his sight. Many of us did. But this would be the first time for me.

A younger man who shared our cabin, Tobias, asked to join me. Broad-bodied, with a solemn nature and a slow smile, he was new to the plantation, having been there only since the start of the harvest season. Tobias bore a bad leg and walked with a limp, but he was a hard worker. He had been ripped away from his family and sought to find them, but he had no bearings on where they were at all. I was uncertain he would find his kinfolk, but I was pleased to have a willing companion, even one who had to drag along his leg.

We waited until the plantation was quiet, late at night, and then we crept into the dark woods beyond the fence. The forbidden lands.

* * *

BENJAMIN LIFTED his teacup to his lips and to his surprise, found the cup empty.

The Negro's colorful narrative was riveting.

If all of it reads like this, this is a certain bestseller, Benjamin thought as he refreshed his tea. His hand shook while he carried the cup back to his chair. He glanced toward the window and saw the full moon cresting the crowns of the pine trees. He ought to have joined Emma in bed, but he yearned to continue with this fascinating tale.

He resumed reading.

* * *

"SOLOMON?" Tobias said. "What in God's name is that?"

It was near dawn. We had journeyed far beyond the farm when we came upon the small clearing in the forest and discovered a spectacle unlike any I had ever seen.

The thing lay at the base of an old, shriveled tree, amongst tangled vines. Waning moonlight cast a pale glow upon it. I saw tiny, luminescent motes floating in the air, like fireflies.

But the fetid stench of death lay heavy in the area, too. I had smelled a dead man before, and this odor brought back that unpleasant memory.

"It's a d-d-d-deer," I said. "A d-d-dead one."

"I ain't never seen no dead deer like that," Tobias said.

I had to agree with him. Something grew out of the deer's innards—long, thick, reddish things that reminded me of ropes. Tentacles, they might have been called in a Greek mythology story like those I had read with the young master. The tentacles grew out of its mouth and ears and ruptured stomach, and all joined together around the tree and the bushes, as if beast and tree had become one.

"It be livin'!" Tobias said. "Look at them eyes, Solomon! They be shinin'!"

The deer's head was twisted and lay against the ground, but its dark eyes glimmered in the moonlight. They reflected an unexpected depth that chilled me, and I thought I saw those eyes blink slowly, too.

What unnatural thing is this? I thought.

Tobias edged forward. Gripped by a fear I couldn't understand, I seized his arm.

"S-s-s-stay away!" I said.

Tobias shook off my hand.

"I wanna see this up close," he said. "I done seen plenty of dead animals, but I ain't seen nothin' like this."

"D-d-d-don't breathe in those f-f-f-fireflies," I said, not knowing what else to call them.

But Tobias limped into the glowing, living haze. At first, he seemed fine, turned back to look at me and grinned, but suddenly, that grin fell off his face and he staggered and sucked in a gasping breath. He collapsed to the ground like a man caught up with a spirit. Lying on the earth, he moaned and writhed, and dark fluids leaked from his mouth.

He breathed it in, I thought. *I told him not to breathe it in!*

I wanted to run. But I couldn't allow him to lie there and suffer. I dug into my sack, pulled out my tattered blanket and wrapped it around my mouth.

Crouched, I moved forward.

I felt the firefly things dancing above my head like warm raindrops. *Don't breathe them in, Solomon!*

That deer watched me with its liquid, fathomless eyes as I got my hands on my friend's trembling leg and dragged him away from the monstrosity. Tobias squirmed and groaned. I pulled him a safe piece away and peeled the blanket away from my mouth. Kneeling, I turned him over to get a good look at him.

Tobias sprang up and vomited black bile into my face.

* * *

I DREAMED ABOUT MARY.

We walked together along the sandy edge of a blue ocean, the warm, golden sun behind our backs. We held hands, and her eyes when she looked at me were like the most precious jewels.

We were home, and we would be there forever...

* * *

I AWOKE to the sound of barking dogs.

I lay on the ground in the cool, dew-dampened grass, pinkish morning sun rays peeking through the trees above. Sitting up, I found myself in a clearing—the same area where we had found the transformed deer. That gruesome thing lay just across the way, its eyes shut. Those tentacles quivered, though, and I understood the creature still lived.

My good sense told me not much time had passed. But I didn't see Tobias.

The last thing I remembered was him spewing black bile into my face. Surely, wherever he was, he was ill. Or dead.

I did not feel like myself, either. The woods seemed more vivid. Colors were brighter. Smells were sharper. Sounds were louder. It was like before this day I had been sleepwalking, and now, I had awakened.

I touched my face where the black sputum had struck me, and I felt a crustiness along my cheeks and jaws, as if fire had licked my skin. I looked at my hands, and I gasped. Purple-black sores scored the length of my arms, and my veins pumped blood as black as ink.

Not fire, I thought. A terrible affliction.

I could not feel my heart beating. I lay my hand against where my damp, soiled shirt covered my chest and felt nothing.

Was I a dead man?

But I had never felt more alive.

* * *

THE BARKING GREW SHARPER. It would be at least four dogs, from what I recalled. The overseer and his two henchmen often trotted those creatures around the plantation, big black hulking animals that reminded me of the Greek myth about Cerberus, the monstrous hound bearing several heads, who guarded the gates of Hades to keep the dead from leaving.

They showed us those dogs to let us know what awaited us if we dared to escape. I had seen a fellow who once tried to run off in the middle of a humid afternoon, and they set those dogs loose and they brought him down and everyone saw it happen. He had never walked right again.

I got up. I should have been afraid, but an odd tingling sensation traveled down my spine.

Ahead, the dogs broke through the dense underbrush. I did

not run—strangely, as I noted, I felt no fear. I stalked toward them.

One of the brutish trackers leading the slavering hounds spotted me.

"There's one of them! Get him, boys!"

He unleashed the dogs and they burst toward me, eyes bright and saliva glistening on their long teeth. But as the dogs drew close, within a stone's throw, they stopped. They tucked their tails between their legs and whimpered and withdrew.

I kept advancing. The tracker cursed the hounds and unlatched a whip from his belt.

"I'll get the nigger myself then!"

As the dogs turned tail and fled, the man charged me, hatred glaring in his eyes, the whip hanging from his fist like a promise.

Something dropped out of the trees and pounced on the tracker. A dark, fast-moving shape.

Tobias.

Only he didn't look quite like the young man I remembered. He had reddened eyes and torn clothes, his skin mapped with blue-black suppurating sores. He landed on the tracker hard enough to break the man's back. Tobias grabbed the man's head in his hands and twisted, cutting off his victim's scream.

Tobias swung toward me. He grinned, his teeth black as mud.

"Tobias, what happened to you?" I asked. Those words flowed from my tongue as swiftly as rain from the sky, as clearly as they were formed in my mind.

My friend's lips did not move but he answered me. I heard his answer in my mind as loudly as I heard my own thoughts.

I'm free, Solomon. We free men now. Don't you feel it? That's what freedom feels like.

I wanted to ask him more, but the other two men neared, the overseer and his other cruel worker. Getting close, they saw

Tobias standing over their fallen companion. The overseer lifted his shotgun and aimed at Tobias.

"Nigger, that's all for you!"

The shotgun boomed, the earth quaking. Buckshot knocked Tobias backward into the tall weeds. I shouted and raced forward, unconcerned for my own safety. I reached for Tobias.

But he was already getting up. Bloodlust flashed in his crimson eyes. Blackish blood peppered his chest, but Tobias seemed unconcerned. His limp had been eradicated, and he moved like a young lion.

I let my hand drop. He did not need my help.

"Finish them!" I said to Tobias.

The overseer gasped, his other brute coming forward with the whip. He snapped it toward Tobias and Tobias grabbed the tip right out of the air and yanked, jerking the man toward him. The man screamed. Tobias drove his fist into the man's stomach with such force that he punctured his innards. They spilled like bloody worms out of his gut. He dropped to the ground with a dying gasp.

"Abomination!" the overseer cried. The shotgun had slipped out of his grasp. "This is the devil's work! Black nigger magic!"

The overseer fled. Tobias swung toward me.

Let's go back, Solomon, he said, without his lips moving. *We can free the others.*

I stepped past Tobias and the two dead men. Sunshine pierced the trees and blistered my eyes, and I edged away from the glare.

"We must wait for the sun to go down," I said.

* * *

BENJAMIN LET the pages settle into his lap. His heart pounded.

"This is a work of fiction," he whispered. Perspiration beaded his temples, though the room was drafty. The Negro had promised every word of this narrative was true, but Benjamin concluded that he had lied. A man could not survive a shotgun wound without suffering a mortal injury. An unarmed Negro could not kill two capable white men and frighten the other to flee.

Pure fiction.

He ought to reject this manuscript, stop reading and join Emma in their warm bed . . . but he reached for the next group of pages, his fingers leaving a damp blot on the edges.

He resumed reading.

* * *

AT NIGHTFALL, we returned to the farm and visited Blind Man Robert. We found him in our old cabin, dry coughs wracking his withered frame. He looked up and squinted blindly when I came through the doorway.

"Solomon?" he asked. "That you?"

"Here we are."

"What y'all doin' here?" He rubbed his eyes. "They been out lookin' for y'all niggahs and y'all done come back?"

"We're here to set you free, brother," I said.

"You smooth talkin' like a white man?" Blind Man Robert blinked.

I gestured toward him, and Tobias shouldered past me and approached our old friend.

Tobias drew in a great breath and exhaled black bile into Blind Man Robert's face. With a cry, the old man tumbled onto the floor. In time, Blind Man Robert rose with the straight-backed posture of a younger man, his eyes glistening like tar.

He looked from me to Tobias.

I can see y'all, he said, but his lips didn't move. Like with

Tobias, I could understand him without him needing to speak a word. Tobias nodded, and I realized Tobias could understand him, too.

I ain't seen since I was a boy, Blind Man Robert told us. He laid his gnarled hand on my shoulder as if confirming I was real.

I clasped his hand.

"You're a free man, like us," I said. "Now, we free us all."

But I didn't understand how this strange condition had changed us. Tobias used to have a limp but now he moved like the wind, and Blind Man Robert now could see, but neither man could speak. Only I could speak, but pushing words off my tongue was formerly my affliction.

If we had died, death had brought us gifts. It was a meager price to pay for freedom.

We crept out of the cabin and visited the others. Blind Man Robert spat the transforming black sputum, too. I had not yet tried it—I was saving mine.

As our fellow slaves gained freedom through death, I wandered, alone, toward the master's mansion, as if led by the mythical siren song. An enormous poplar tree grew in the grassy front yard. As I neared that tree, I smelled something —men.

I turned, but too late.

"He's the main one!" Master cried. He had blackened his face with soot to hide his paleness.

A noose fell over my head.

* * *

BOTH OF THEIR faces darkened with coal, Master and the overseer tugged the rope they had hoisted over the poplar tree. It snatched me off the ground, the loop tightening around my neck. Mania blazed in the overseer's eyes.

"Black nigger magic ain't gonna save you from a hangin', boy!" the overseer said.

"I was good to you, Solomon!" Master said, saliva frothing on his pink lips. "You repay me with an uprising?"

I kicked my legs and jerked about. I couldn't breathe. The rope on my neck burned like the time I was branded, as a boy. I had never felt such pain in the body. I looked up at the dark sky and felt the blackness coming down like jaws swallowing me.

I thought about Mary. Her eyes like precious jewels and her sunshine smile. Her last words to me surfaced in my mind.

It's gonna be all right, Solomon. We gonna see each other again.

I thought about a slave I had once known. I was young and don't remember his name, but I remembered his remarkable size and strength and courage. Once he had endured a brutal whipping at the overseer's hands that I had witnessed from across the yard, and he didn't make a noise, didn't cry out or shed a tear, and when he shuffled back to the cabins, sweating and dripping blood, I remember him pointing to his large skull and saying: *I ain't think 'bout no pain, so I ain't feel it. It's all up in here in your head, y'all.*

All up here in your head...

I raised my hands and seized the rope around my neck.

I couldn't breathe.

But I didn't need to breathe anymore.

And the pain I felt was all in my head.

I didn't need to feel pain anymore, either.

I tore myself loose and dropped to the earth.

"GODDAMN!" the overseer said, backing away. "It ain't natural!"

"Devilry," Master said, his eyes wide.

Both men turned to flee, but by then, my companions had

arrived. A few of them carried torches they could have only gotten by breaking into the plantation's forbidden supply sheds. I smelled the rich, sweet fragrance of tobacco wafting through the night air. My friends were setting the fields afire.

Now, they seized the overseer and Master. Both men had dealt cruelly with us, but only Master interested me.

"Where is my Mary?" I asked him.

Master spat at me. "Burn in hell, nigger!"

Someone splashed pungent oil on our captors. Another friend laid the torch on their soaked clothes and flesh. Flames erupted in a mighty conflagration.

Burn in hell, indeed.

Their howls of torment echoed around me as I trod toward Master's stately home. I pushed open the door and walked through it—I had never seen a Negro go inside through that door, only through an entry in the back. The master reserved the front entrance for white men.

But the acrid odor of burning cash crops thickened the air inside these wide, polished corridors, too. Candles glowed along the hallway. I neared a mirror edged in gold and paused, gazed into my reflection.

I am, indeed, a dead man, I realized as I looked upon myself. I touched my face.

"Don't you move, mister," a woman's voice said.

In the mirror, I saw a figure approach behind me. A pale woman wearing a flowing white nightgown.

She held a rifle, but her hands trembled on it.

I turned to face the master's wife. She took a step back, her lips quivering.

"Mary said you were kind to her," I said. "We will spare your life if you tell me who purchased Mary."

The woman sucked in her bottom lip. Her gaze flicked

toward the front door. The wails of her husband and the overseer continued to echo through the night.

"Do you promise?" Tears slid down her cheeks. "My children..."

"Tell me where Mary has been taken."

She lowered the rifle and led me into another room. It was a space laden with bookcases and the head of a mounted deer looking down upon us. I reflected on the strange deer we had come upon in the woods, in my old life.

The study also had a large oak desk, a lantern glowing atop it.

"He kept his business papers in that drawer." She pointed at the desk.

I pulled open the drawer and found a stack of printed documents.

"But . . . can you read?" she asked.

I only grinned at her.

* * *

BENJAMIN HAD REACHED the final page of Solomon's narrative. It contained only a few sentences. He read it, his blood running cold as a stream in January. He rubbed his eyes and read it again.

I have located the man who purchased my wife, Mr. Benjamin Parker. Do you now understand why I chose you? Bring my Mary to our meeting. Do this and I will trouble you no more. I have left you this narrative as a testament to the reckoning promised for those men who dare to enslave other men.

Cursing, Benjamin ripped the last page to shreds.

* * *

THE NEXT MORNING, after a restless night of sleep, Benjamin made inquiries in town.

He sought to confirm the truth of Solomon's tale. The local slave patrol authorities did not know of any recent, successful slave uprisings in Virginia. When he pressed them, they asked him for details, which sent him back to Solomon's manuscript.

But Solomon's fanciful tale contained no information that he could share with the patrol: he hadn't named the plantation owner, overseer, or any of the whites. He hadn't named the farm property or given a precise location. The events might have occurred anywhere in the state—or nowhere at all except in the Negro's fevered imagination.

He's played me for a fool, Benjamin thought. *Well, I'll show him. I'll put him in his proper place.*

At the appointed time, the evening of the third day since his encounter with the lying Negro, Benjamin waited in his office. He had alerted the slave patrol that a runaway Negro was due to appear. Two armed men waited outside the building on horses.

Benjamin looked outside the window at the patrol and smiled.

I will have the last word on this matter, Solomon, he thought.

Dusk arrived, but Solomon did not appear. Soon, there was a knock at the door. It was the lead slave patrol officer.

"I think we scared that nigger away," the ruddy-faced man said.

"Evidently," Benjamin said.

The man frowned at Benjamin. "You still can't tell us what farm he ran off from?"

"He lied to me." Benjamin felt blood flush his cheeks.

"That's what they do, friend—lie." The patrol shook his head and chuckled, as if amused at Benjamin's naivete. "We're heading home, mister. If you see that nigger again you let us know."

As the patrol departed, Benjamin returned to his desk. He had piled Solomon's fictional narrative atop it, next to a candle match. He had intended to make quite the show if the Negro had dared to arrive. Reckoning indeed!

He packed his things, preparing to return home.

Someone knocked on the door again: three quick raps.

Had the patrol returned to mock him further? Sighing, Benjamin stomped across the room and flung the door open.

No one was there.

But a silver necklace lay on the threshold, glittering in the dimming sunlight.

Oh, no. My wife.

* * *

BENJAMIN RUSHED HOME.

He was in too much of a hurry to alert the authorities, and most of all, cautious of allowing the Negro to make a fool of him again if Benjamin raised another alarm that proved false. *He is playing a game with me, but I will win this match.*

It was full dark when Benjamin arrived at his residence. Lamp light glowed in the front windows. The house was the portrait of pastoral tranquility.

But Benjamin's anxiety didn't ease until he entered and found Emma safe with their three children in the drawing room, reading a book. The delicious aromas of a simmering meal wafted from the kitchen.

"My dear, what's the matter?" Emma asked. "You look frightened, Benny."

"Your necklace." He drew it out of his pocket and dangled it in front of her.

Emma's eyes widened, and she touched her bare neck.

"I had been looking for my necklace," she said. "Where did you find it?"

"It was stolen. Have you seen anyone around the house today? Specifically, a Negro male?"

"Do you suspect Solomon was here?" Terror shone in her eyes. Benjamin had confided everything in his wife.

Benjamin heard a dish shatter. He spun.

Mary, their maidservant, wandered into the doorway of the drawing room. Normally, the sweet-tempered Negro woman never met Benjamin's eyes, but her gaze bored into him so deeply that he felt as if she'd lanced him with a sewing needle.

"My Solomon be here?" Mary asked, hands wringing her apron.

Benjamin drew his pistol from his jacket pocket. It was a Colt .45 that he had rarely fired. But it was loaded—he'd been carrying it on his person since learning of Solomon's deceit.

"A *thief* may be here," he said. "Emma, stay in here with the children. You," He nodded toward Mary, "return to your quarters."

"Mister . . . if my Solomon be here, I wanna see him," Mary said. Steel flashed in her eyes.

Benjamin stammered, his childhood stutter resurfacing. "Y-y-y-you . . . b-b-b-better obey m-m-m-me!"

But Mary whirled and fled from the room. Benjamin hurried after her into the main corridor, clutching the pistol so tightly it might have been glued to his palm.

How dare this Negro woman disobey his command? She was in *his* employ. She did not know her place. He would teach her *and* Solomon a lesson.

Mary flung open the front door. Standing on the threshold, she let out a soft cry—Benjamin couldn't tell if it was joy, or horror, but his knees felt watery as he edged toward her. He looked out into the night.

A dark legion surrounded his residence. There might have been twenty, or thirty, or more. He did not know. He could not count them. The part of his mind that adroitly performed calculations had shut down as he gazed upon these things that could not be men or women—unless men and women could rise from the grave and walk.

Solomon emerged from the center of the horde. He no longer wore the concealing kerchief he had worn upon his initial visit to Benjamin's office. He had removed the grubby cap, too. His face was fully revealed, in all its horror.

My Lord in Heaven, Benjamin thought.

But without thinking, he shoved the pistol's muzzle into Mary's ribcage. The woman yelped.

"She belongs to me!" Benjamin said. "I paid six hundred dollars for her!"

Solomon raised his hand and pointed at Benjamin. "What would you pay for the lives of your wife and children?"

The horde stirred, agitated at the mere suggestion of Solomon's words. Their dark eyes flashed in anticipation of violence. Benjamin's stomach tightened.

The pistol felt like a lead weight in his hand. He lowered it to his side.

With a soft sob, Mary stepped forward, descended the stairs, and slid into Solomon's embrace. She clutched him tightly. Solomon parted his lips and pressed his mouth to hers. The woman convulsed, as if caught in a seizure.

The black sputum, Benjamin thought. *But...it was a tale of fiction!*

Carrying Mary, Solomon sank into the protective folds of the dark horde. As though they were under the influence of a hive mind, the group receded like a silent, black wave into the woods.

Benjamin swallowed thickly. Emma touched his arm. He hadn't realized she was near.

"Was that Solomon?" She sounded out of breath.

Benjamin didn't answer, not trusting himself to speak.

"Are you going to publish his narrative, Benny?"

Benjamin gazed toward the dark, dark woods beyond his property.

"No man will believe it," he whispered.

"But *you* believe."

Benjamin looked at his wife, and for the first time since he was a child, he cried.

The End

INHERITANCE

L. MARIE WOOD

To his credit, the attempt had been a good one. He'd called Hattie into service faster than she'd been able to find a suitable slave. The argument had really burned him up, so he went home that night and set to the business of concocting his potion. But Hattie had been easy to dissuade, at least thus far. Sharon didn't have to do much more than lock the door against her to keep her at bay. A quick side-step and the old girl was lost. Wilson hadn't bothered to teach Hattie anything more than how to get up and walk again. He told her to go after Sharon and to kill her, but he hadn't told her how.

Sharon got used to the beating against her front door. Hattie could stay out there all night if she wanted to. It didn't bother Sharon any and there wasn't a neighbor to complain about the noise for miles. She figured Wilson would wait until morning to see if Hattie had done the job. At least until after the funeral, just so it would look right. People would wonder why he wasn't in the family car, it being his brother-in-law's funeral and all. They would wonder why he would be anywhere except right by his wife's side.

Sharon had time.

Hattie hadn't figured out that she would do better to bust in the windows. Sharon doubted she would. The woman hadn't been a brain surgeon in life. How could she be expected to do better in death? Sharon sucked her teeth as she walked into the spare bathroom, the room where she brewed her potions and cast her spells. She thought back on how they had gotten to the place they were now--wanting to rip each other limb from limb as soon as look at one another.

Their mother had left the shop to both of them. She had been a respected woman in their village, a woman who was known to take care of people's problems. Half the time she didn't do anything except sell roots and dried fruit for one potion or the next; she told Sharon and Wilson herself that the whole thing was bogus. But it worked, and she never had to put in a hard day's labor in the hot sun in her life.

Wilson played around with it, 'Momma's mumbo-jumbo' he called it. He was the oldest and the one who was supposed to inherit the business. He never caught on though, and was easily overshadowed by his younger sister, who seemed to have the real gift. When their mother died, she left everything to the both of them. And that's where the trouble started.

"You're making us look like fools," Sharon said, from the back room of the shop that day. "No one will believe us if you keep gallivanting around the street like a commoner."

"They don't believe us as it is, Sharon," he said, tired of the argument. It was always the same thing over and over. "People are smarter now. They know this is a bunch of bullshit."

Sharon burst through the beads that hung from the ceiling to separate the rooms and growled, "Watch your tongue in momma's house."

Wilson chuckled. "Sharon, momma's been dead for ten years already. When are you gonna cut it out?" He turned his back to his sister and touched one of the dry herbs that hung from the ceiling.

"Her *ánimo* is still here, Wilson. She's angry that you speak of her that way."

"Right, sure," he said condescendingly. "Anyhow, I just came here to tell you that I'll be talking with a man about selling this dump. I'm gonna try and get whatever money we can out of this place and do something with it. Maybe I'll move to the mainland. Who knows?"

Sharon looked stricken. "You can't sell the place! This is momma's legacy!"

Wilson flicked the herb and sent it swinging on the string. "It's not much of a legacy, now is it? We can barely live on what we make from it. I have to work a second job just to keep food on the table." He shook his head and stood to leave. "I'm selling it, Sharon. And there's nothing you can do about it."

Wilson walked toward the door, opened it, and turned to speak before leaving. "But you should have already known that, *bruja*."

Sharon cursed him then, vowing to stop him by any means necessary. She didn't utter a sound as she stood facing the closed door of her mother's shop, but Wilson heard every word.

The church was sticky, and the mosquitoes relentless. They couldn't resist the bounty they were getting: thirty people crammed in a small church with nothing but their hands to protect them. They feasted.

Wilson escorted his wife in and sat in front of the body of her brother. Clay had been a strong man, muscular and fit for most of his life, but that didn't save him. He worked out on the boats and was stung by a Portuguese Man of War during an afternoon pull. They didn't make it back to the dock in time to save him after he went into cardiac arrest.

As his wife sobbed, all Wilson could think about was Sharon.

She wasn't at the funeral, so she must be dead. Sharon wouldn't have missed Clay's service. She fancied him and was genuinely saddened by his death. Wilson tried to conceal his smile as he thought of Hattie taking Sharon by surprise. She must have been shocked to see her, considering she had attended Hattie's funeral a couple of days earlier. Wilson would talk to the man after they put Clay in the ground, he decided. He would have his money in less than a month.

His wife's shaking grew intense and a cry was stuck in her throat, choking her.

Wilson turned to her. "Honey? Honey, are you ok?"

He didn't see Clay fidgeting in his tight casket, didn't recognize the sounds of grunting from his chest and the ripping of the stitches in his lips to be what they were.

His wife's eyes were wide open, unblinking, in shock.

"Honey?" He shook her slightly, trying to get her attention and pull her out of the day terror. She wouldn't look at him.

Wilson turned his head in the direction of his wife's stare in time to see Clay sit up in the casket. An audible moan escaped his chest as the air escaped his lungs. Clay forced his mouth and eyes open, ripping what was left of the stitches apart. He lifted his right arm and then his left, inspecting them in disbelief. The whole thing was so much déjà vu to Wilson, he couldn't move.

Then Clay climbed out of the casket.

Wilson didn't hear the shrieks and screams emanating from the congregation as Clay planted his feet on the floor. He only saw Sharon standing at the back of the church smiling prettily, devilishly.

Clay moved fastfor one of the undead. He closed the space between himself and Wilson in three strides and pressed down on his shoulders, buckling his legs, making him submit. Wilson became aware of a pungent odor, the smell of meat that had been left out in the sun. Sharon had converted Hattie in the light of day and brought her along as backup.

With everything he could remember from Momma, with everything he had, he called Hattie inside. She came sluggishly, bewildered. She looked at Sharon who was too busy watching the show in front of her to notice. Then she looked at Wilson.

He intimated his command to her, deftly breaking Sharon's spell and reinforcing his own. Hattie was upon Sharon before she could turn around. He wished she had; Wilson would've loved to have seen the look of surprised terror on Sharon's face.

I'm better than you now, sister. I bloomed right under your nose.

The smell of fresh blood permeated the air as Hattie ripped away Sharon's scalp. Sharon's scream was nothing more than an afterthought as was her limp hand against Hattie's decaying cheek. She was dead as soon as her skull was exposed to the summer air. Hattie banged Sharon's head against the wall like a squirrel might a nut and pawed at the brain inside.

Clay smelled the blood just before Wilson did. He turned his head, loosening his grip just enough for Wilson to slip away. Clay lunged at Sharon, grabbing her leg and digging his nails into her skin, cutting through the flesh and muscle with determined swipes. He licked at the blood spewing from the wounds before baring his teeth and biting into the supple flesh. Wilson slinked against the wall, trying to make a quiet exit while Hattie and Clay dined on Sharon. He noticed for the first time that the church was empty; everyone had fled, running for their lives, including his wife. He'd have to remember that she hadn't tried to help him at all she had just left him there to deal with two zombies. Yes, that was useful information indeed.

Wilson stood in the doorway to watch as Clay sank his teeth into Sharon for another bite, sinews and fatty tissue draped over his working lips. He looked at Sharon's face one last time, at her ruined eyes and what was left of her exposed brain and smiled.

As he closed the door to the church, his expression transformed from grim satisfaction to abject fear to please the waiting crowd. His wife ran up to him, tears streaming from her eyes, wetting her cheeks. He hugged her hurriedly, burying his face in her welcoming neck, deftly hiding the hatred in his eyes.

He'd meet the man later that day.

He'd have his money in less than a month.

The End

DEAD MAN COUNTRY

STEVEN VAN PATTEN

To say that Roberta was taken aback by the contestant's appearance and odor is an understatement. Dumbfounded, it took a full seven seconds to find her voice.

"Hello. I'm Roberta. I'm one of the stage managers. I'm here to take you to stage, Mr. Nail."

"Then I'm much obliged to you, Roberta!" Nail answered as he stood up from the green room's loveseat and slipped on his weathered, gothic, black leather jacket. "Can I leave my guitar case in here?"

"Sh-Sh-sure." Roberta stammered.

Nail slung his 1955 Gretsch acoustic guitar over his back. The way the neck stuck out over the left side of his back was reminiscent of the way a movie samurai's katana might be worn. Nail followed the stage manager through the door and down a corridor that led to a series of black curtains. As they walked past a group of stagehands and other theater staff gathered against the left side of the walkway, he greeted their looks of fear and revulsion with a nod and a polite tip of his cowboy hat.

Roberta cast an occasional look over her shoulder, seemingly caught between making sure Nail was still behind her and avoiding eye contact at all costs. Especially since there seemed to be a missing eyelid.

When they'd parted the last thick black drape at stage right, they could finally see inside the theater. "Just take that seat on that stool centerstage. The judges and producers are in the audience. They'll take it from here. Good luck." The stage manager pointed the way before hustling back behind the curtain.

"Thank you, very much." Nail nodded as he stepped forward.

The air in the three-hundred-person maximum capacity theater was stuffy, but the interior was colorful. Plush burgundy seats and spots of either pale-blue or fire orange lighting splashed across paintings and sculptures. Nail's cowboy boots sounded like doors slamming as he strode to the stool and microphone. Once seated in a solitary pool of white light, his pupils dilated in their nearly uncovered sockets as he looked out into the seats.

"Should I just begin?" Nail's first words boomed through the theater speakers.

With the nearly blinding intensity of the stage lights, he could barely make out the features of the three celebrity judges seated at a long, unlacquered table squeezed in between the second and third rows, but he could tell they were recoiling even at this distance.

"Um—Hello. I'm Chet. I think maybe we could talk a little first," A man's shaky voice answered from the shadows.

"That's fine," he said as he positioned the guitar onto his knee. "And I know who you are. Five-time Grammy and six-time CMT winner, Chet Howard. Just as I would've had to have been dead a long time not to know who the legendary Miriam Hatfield and Will Ryder are as well. Platinum artists, all of you. Anyway, what would you like to talk about, sir?"

"I guess we could start with you telling us your name and where you're from," Miriam's voice called out. She sounded almost as nervous as Chet.

"My name is Rusty C. Nail, and I'm from Coosa County, Alabama."

Will Ryder suspected this entire encounter was some sort of prank. When he spoke, he sounded decidedly suspicious. "I must admit that's quite the get-up, Mr. Nail. You have a friend that does special effects make-up, or did you do this yourself? You a method actor, by chance?"

"Mr. Ryder, sir, if you are referring to my undead visage, I feel I should inform you that my appearance is by no means a fabrication, an act or 'special effects' as you say. The only part of me that is a performance is what I do with this here *gee-tar*."

The three judges whispered among themselves as the staff scattered throughout the theater collectively gasped and in hushed tones shared speculations to one another. Finally, Will Ryder asked, "Sir, why exactly do you want to be on 'America's Next Country Star'?"

"Well, I thought that'd be obvious," Rusty said. "But the short answer is now that I find myself an immortal, I need that there prize money y'all are offering like a snake needs rats."

"Yes, but you're here now asserting that you want to be on the show and that you're, in fact, a zombie?"

"Zombie-American," Rusty corrected.

"Oh yes, forgive me!" Will said with hands held up in surrender. "It's just that I'm new to the whole supernatural creatures being real and auditioning to be on a television show to boot. May I ask, were you a part of a government experiment or are you just a harbinger of the End of Days?"

"Neither, to my knowledge," Rusty answered. "I came about my condition the ol' fashioned way."

"You were bitten by a zombie?" the lady asked.

"No! The *other* ol' fashioned way," Rusty answered. "And zombies don't bite people who ain't asking to get bit. That there is one of them racist stereotypes perpetuated by Hollywood."

"So... witch doctor?" Chet volunteered.

Rusty sighed. "Okay, the *very* old-fashioned way. I was, in fact, kicked out of heaven."

More whispering at the judge's table. The only thing Rusty could make out for sure was when one of the producers said something about him having a 'face for radio and a body odor for Staten Island.'

One of the producers separated from the pack inside the theater and stood next to the judges' table. He wore a very typical pair of blue jeans and light blue shirt. His sleeves were rolled up revealing a Rolex that succeeded in both telling time and screaming, *I've won some Emmys.*

"Sir, I don't mean any disrespect, but could you explain what you mean by being 'kicked out of heaven'."

Rusty smiled. His red eyes, peeling skin and dark yellow teeth all seemed to shine in the spotlight's beam. "I'm more than happy to explain, Mr. TV Producer Man." He quickly tuned one string on the Gretsch and took a deep breath as long, brown, jagged fingernails found the guitar strings.

Well, I died and went to Heaven
And some thought that was wrong
Cause the way I was livin'
Was sinnin' pretty strong

But a sweet little angel messed up
And opened the gates for me
Then the saints found out
And they're not lettin' me be

Lord have mercy,
They're coming to take my wings
Lord have mercy,
They're coming to take my wings
Don't wanna go to the other place
Cause hellfire sure does sting
Lord have mercy,
They're coming to take my wings

Lost track of how long I was there
Pretendin' I'm an angel
The only good thing I'd done since
Is help this whore named Mabel
I like my whiskey and my gin
Up there, guess that's a crime
Cause Gabe's blowing his trumpet
And Pete said I'm outta time!

Lord have mercy,
They're coming to take my wings
Lord have mercy,
They're coming to take my wings
Don't wanna go to the other place
Cause hellfire sure does sting
Lord have mercy,
They're coming to take my wings

Well sure enough they kicked me out
Didn't even say goodbye
Figured I'd end up in hell
Where my soul would surely die
But I guess that favor I did Mabel
Earned me a breather

Cause now I'm walking dead on Earth,
Cause hell don't want me neither!

Lord have mercy,
They came and took my wings
Lord have mercy,
They came and took my wings
I'm back and I'm a zombie
But at least I still can sing
Lord have mercy,
They came and took my wings!

Won over by Rusty's emotional delivery and perfect pitch, everyone present gave Nail a thunderous round of applause. Once it died down, Miriam cheered through her broad smile. "Rusty C. Nail! We will see you in Memphis!"

As the crowd continued to whoop and holler, Nail realized Miriam must be the one in charge. He pushed the stool back and stood up.

"Much obliged, ma'am. Gentlemen," he said with another tip of his hat as he slung the guitar back over his shoulder and sauntered back to stage right.

Once Nail exited, the judges and producers turned to each other.

"Miriam, are you seriously putting him on air?" Chet asked. "We're going to need a friggin' parental advisory warning before he performs!"

"I think he's going to make great television, advisory or not," Miriam answered as she turned to the third producer. "Make it happen, Brad!"

Brad The Producer rolled his eyes as he pulled his cellphone from his jacket pocket. "I just hope getting him on a plane isn't going to be the pigfuck I think it will be," he said before turning his attention to his phone call. "Hey Cynthia! Have the PAs pick up air freshener. No, a whole bunch. All kinds. Just have them clean out the Walgreen's on Fifth Avenue. And when you are done with that, call Elise from make-up. Let her know she is going to need a lot of foundation in Memphis and maybe two fake eyelids. I know it doesn't make sense now, but it will when you see him.

* * *

GILBERT HAD ASKED HIS WIFE, Alli, to keep things quiet so he could take a nap and be sharp for work later in the evening. That request, like many he'd made during his ten-year marriage, would end up being ignored.

"You lied to me!" she thundered down at him as he blinked sleep away.

Gilbert sat up. "For the love of God, woman! I'm working tonight!"

"Yes, I know, oh great zombie killer! At least that's what you tell me you're doing."

Gilbert had been sitting on the bed but stood and faced his wife. "That is exactly what I'm doing."

"Well, I dunno! You could be lying about that too."

"What is it with you?" He could feel his temper about to give way. "I have never lied to you about anything."

"Tell that to the zombie on *America's Next Country Star*."

"WHAT?"

Barely giving Gilbert a chance to move his legs, Alli pulled her laptop from under her arm and sat down hard on the bed. As Gilbert repositioned himself so he could sit next to her, she furiously typed until a YouTube page appeared.

"This is what I'm talking about!" she said as she turned the volume all the way up and hit the triangle-shaped icon next to the word PLAY.

The initially blank screen filled with a 'TV-14' logo, as a voiceover kicked in: "The following segment of America's Next Country Star may be disturbing to some viewers. Parents may opt to have smaller children sit this one out."

The 'TV-14' logo faded into blackness, soon to be replaced by the *America's Next Country Star* red, blue, and gold logo, which after a few seconds, whisked away out of frame revealing Harpy Collins, the blonde, buxom MC of the show. Behind her, a seated audience of three-hundred people cheered and applauded.

"Welcome back to America's Next Country Star! Now I need to prepare you folks at home for our next contestant, because he is something of an original. Rusty C. Nail, who hails from Coosa County, Alabama is not your typical singer, or even your typical human being. In fact, he identifies as a true-to-life Zombie-American. Yes, I find it hard to believe as well. Like most of you I'm sure, I've never met a zombie before. But folks, I'll tell ya, he is backstage, live, in the flesh. Sort of. Now, I'm not gonna mince words! Rusty might be a little hard on the eyes. But he has an amazing voice, and he is here to compete. Now, before we bring him out, here is a look at what transpired when he auditioned!"

As the show cut to an abridged version of Rusty's interview with the judges before he started singing, a shocked Gilbert jumps to his feet.

Alli sneered. "Oh, don't act all surprised!"

"Honey, this must be a guy in make-up! Zombies can't even talk, much less sing! This guy's a fraud!"

She rolled her eyes. "Whatever."

They continued to watch as the program cut back to Nashville, Harpy Collins, and her enthusiastically cheering audience.

"Ladies and gentlemen, put your hands together for a real-life embodiment of proof of the existence of God! Rusty C. Nail, with his original song, 'Dead Man Country'!"

The camera flies over Harpy's head, the shot closing in on the stage. There Rusty sits alone on a stool as he did in the audition, his glistening guitar mounted on his lap.

In the show's control room, the director called out a reminder to his camera operators. "All right everyone, just like we talked about in the meeting, let's play this one kinda loose!"

Close-ups or no close-ups, Gilbert saw enough of Rusty's complexion to know that he was in fact the real deal. "Good grief!"

"Anything you wanna tell me?" Alli snapped.

"No dear." He sounded contrite even though he'd done nothing wrong.

They listened to the lyrics intently, especially the part about Rusty being kicked out of heaven.

"Is that what happens to these poor souls?" Alli asked. "They get kicked out of heaven and you and your people persecute and kill them? And where do they go after you and your thug friends kill them a second time?"

As the song ended, his cellphone buzzed. Grabbing it off the nightstand to his right, he saw that it was RAYMOND calling. "Honey, I have to take this."

"I bet." She huffed as she watched him walk out.

In the bedroom doorway he finally answered the call. "Raymond?"

"Thank God!" the relieved voice answered. "Did you see what happened?"

"If you're talking about the singing zombie on national fucking TV, well then, yes!"

"You have to take care of it!"

The urgency in Raymond's voice was not enough for Gilbert. "What the fuck are you talking about? Why me?"

"You're in West Virginia! You're the closest."

Gilbert groaned. "Fuck me! How did this even happen?"

"I don't know, dude! The best I can say is they seem to have evolved."

"Evolved overnight into country western stars? You're kidding right?"

"I don't have another explanation! But I need you to take care of this before I lose my funding."

"Funding? For the love of Christ, why would the funding get pulled?"

Raymond sighed. "Well, to be fair, I was not honest with you about where the funding comes from."

There goes the honesty thing again. "What do you mean? You said you were government funded."

"That is kind of true. But it's the vampire government."

Gilbert's eyes grew wide as his head whipped back to see whether Alli overheard Wilson through the phone's bleed through. Thankfully, she was still watching the show, listening to Miriam Hatfield gushing over Rusty's singing. "The what government?"

"Vampires." Now it was Raymond's turn to sound contrite. "My family has had a relationship with their leader for decades. It started when I was a kid. He saved my father and me from muggers, then I snuck out of the house to check on him because I thought he was hurt."

"You snuck out of the house to save a vampire?"

Raymond sounded irritated. "Yes! Only the exertion gave me an asthma attack. He took me to the hospital and called my father. After that, he became a family friend."

"Why didn't you tell me this before?"

"Because it was irrelevant to your situation! You needed to

get out of New York after your little gambling thing. So, I introduced you to zombie-hunting for hire and moved you to West Virginia because that was where an outbreak was! And zombies have been popping up there ever since and you were being paid handsomely. You didn't need to know about Christian."

"Well, now I know!" Gilbert insisted. "So, it was this vampire who just put you in charge of zombie disposal?"

"It's complicated, but Christian used to be sort of a vampire cop. Used to kill a lot of werewolves. Vampires oversee making sure the human public stays oblivious to the fact that all those monsters you see in the movies do exist. But there was some infighting and he kind of became like their president or something. Then, his political enemies found out he had a whole family of Puerto Ricans that knew everything. He was able to convince the vampire nation not to kill us, but only because he was able to prove that we've known what he was since the 1970s and never mentioned anything to anyone who wasn't immediate family."

Gilbert interrupted. "Wait a minute! You mean the king or president or whatever of vampires is Puerto Rican?!"

"Nah! He's black! Been around since slavery! Shit is wild."

Gilbert shook his head in disbelief. *The leader of the world's vampires is a black guy from slavery times? How are me and every white person in creation not dead or enslaved?*

"Well, he's not going to kill you, is he?"

"That depends on how quickly we can address this, which is why I already booked you on a very early flight. I will PayPal you some money for expenses and have a guy that will be waiting for you at the airport with some weapons."

"Weapons? He's in the middle of shooting a TV show! How am I supposed to get next to him?"

"I will see what I can procure on my end as far as a fake ID and an exit strategy are concerned. But the main thing is to get you on the ground."

Gilbert sighed. "You're going to owe me big at the end of this! I mean it."

If you survive. "I know, Gilbert. I know."

Gilbert ended the call and braced himself for Alli's reaction to his having to leave for Nashville. She was never one for surprises.

* * *

THE CALLER ID in his cellphone read, UNKNOWN, but he knew who it was.

"Lord Christian!"

"Hello, Raymond," The voice was both familiar and slightly annoyed. "And you don't have to call me, 'Lord'."

Nervousness crept into his voice. "Sure, Christian,"

Christian Brookwater, the Lord of Vampires, seated at his desk in a relatively newly built Manhattan skyscraper, leaned back in his sumptuous burgundy leather office chair. "I take it you know why I'm calling."

"I saw the program, yes."

Christian took a deep breath. "I need a full report. Is this Rusty Nail really a zombie?"

"Naturally, I am hoping this is a fake. But I'll have a man on the ground in Nashville by tomorrow morning."

Christian's voice raised. "I hope you understand how very serious this is. I mean, werewolves were always my problem until we figured out a way to broker a truce. Other vampires were always in charge of catching the cemetery runners..."

"Catching the who?" Raymond asked.

"Cemetery runners," Christian repeated. "That's vampire slang for zombies."

"Oh!"

"Anyway, we never did put enough effort into figuring out why people occasionally rise up to be animated corpses with a taste for human flesh. That's our mistake, I guess. We were focused on the symptoms and not the problem."

"Yes!" he may have agreed too strongly. "But not to worry, I'll get rid of the singing cowboy zombie."

"I want him brought in alive."

"I'm sorry?" He felt suddenly dizzy. "You want him alive, you said?"

"You know what I mean!" Christian realized the mistake in his wording. "I want him brought in in his animated state. No final death. How else am I supposed to figure out how they've evolved from wandering around aimlessly attacking people to being fully cognizant and performing country music on TV?"

"Okay, I'll let Gilbert know."

"Gilbert?" Christian sounded uneasy with that revelation. "The one with the gambling problem?"

"He's been clear for a while now," he answered. "He's been doing a great job in West Virginia and he's the closest one in my network."

"Understood," Christian said. "Keep me in the loop."

"Of course."

Christian ended the call, then punched up another. "Hey. We're going to need a few things. A very recently deceased white guy in his thirties, for one. We are in New York, so hopefully a corpse will materialize naturally, but if forced to murder someone... you know how we do it. Find a child molester or something."

A woman's voice answered. "Check."

"Next, find a good special effects make-up artist. Then, get yourself, and those two things in Nashville as soon as possible. Use the private jet to stay ahead and try to beat the commercial flights. I'll deal with the other thing here at home. And tell Stephen to call me. I have an assignment for him and his computer lab friends."

He ended the second call and slumped down in his seat. After a moment, a single tear fell from the vampire lord's left eye.

"Damn you, Raymond."

* * *

EVEN THOUGH RUSTY came in second place in the first round of the competition, no one outside of the judges congratulated him at the afterparty. In fact, once everyone from the show settled inside the Memphis Westin's bar and lounge, no one spoke to him at all. Rusty would find himself alone, quietly nursing a whiskey and water in far a corner, while everyone else reveled over how well things went. The lighting director laughed with the camera guys. Various producers huddled in their west coast and east coast cliques of three or four gossiping about God only knows. Harpy Collins and Miriam Hatfield carried on a hushed conversation at the far end of the bar, while judges Chet Howard and Will Ryder stood chatting at the other end, each flanked by their respective wives. The ladies both knew better than to allow their rich, handsome, and famous husbands to roam the hotel without them. Only the stagehands were missing, because they were all locals who lived in Memphis and had gone home to their families.

Finally, it was Brad the producer who sauntered over and took a seat on a nearby ottoman. "You know, technically you shouldn't be here. You may be undead, or whatever, but you're still a contestant. Can't let it get out that you're swaying the judges with your dazzling personality."

"But doesn't the winner get chosen by people calling in?" Rusty squinted with the one eye that had a full eyelid.

"True, but they're still the ones who must comment on your performance, and it is that commentary that often sways the voting. Someone is liable to say the judges were swayed by the charming zombie's gift of gab."

"But no one is talking to me," Rusty countered.

"All the more reason you should go back to your room." Brad rose to his feet, suddenly standing over Rusty like a schoolteacher sending a ten-year-old to the principal's office.

Eat him!

"Okay, Brad. Guess I'll see you tomorrow."

More than a few of the partyers noticed Rusty get up from his chair, pick up his whiskey, and make his way to the elevator banks.

As he disappeared behind the closing doors, Miriam excused herself from Harpy and made her way to Brad. "What did you say to him?"

"Just that he shouldn't be down here commiserating with us," Brad explained. "Do you see any of the living contestants here?"

Miriam rolled her eyes. "Don't get flippant with me, Brad! You know I have a no asshole policy as far as the staffing goes." She said his name as if it were an insult.

"And need I remind you that I am also beholden to the network Miriam," Brad countered with a slight neck roll and a good dose of venom while saying her name.

Miriam's eyes lit with anger. "Look here, you little New York Queen! I don't care whose dick you're sucking on, I'm the executive producer. And as such, I had better not catch you ever saying anything cross to him again. You hear me! I don't care what he is under there, let it be a zombie or Kenny Rogers himself."

It wasn't lost on Brad that people were starting to notice he was being publicly chastised, even if no one was close enough to hear the conversation. "Does this have anything to do with your little Christian Church Group trying to book time with Rusty?"

Her widening eyes were a giveaway. "Goddamn your heathen, New York ass! Rusty Nail is living, breathing, walking proof of God!"

"Maybe," Brad nodded. "But I've been speaking to some people and as far as they're concerned, a zombie is a zombie! He could start killing us at any minute or biting us and then we're all wandering the theater slowly decomposing."

"He's perfectly safe," Miriam said. "I've seen it in those soulful eyes of his. That song of his. He's telling the truth! I bet my life on it."

"You've already bet the show on it, Miriam!" Brad snapped. "And if he hurts someone…"

"Stop it, already!"

"…it'll be on your head because you had an agenda outside of finding a country star."

Brad walked away, leaving Miriam standing in the middle of the bar looking furious, while everyone else pretended nothing was out of the ordinary.

* * *

BECAUSE HIS FINGERS weren't warm enough, Rusty always struggled to answer his cellphone. "Hello?"

He heard a familiar voice. "Just called to congratulate you."

"Yes, thank you," Rusty smiled sheepishly. "Only thing is, I don't think some of these people like me very much."

"They'll like you plenty once you win."

"I suppose." Rusty sighed. "Sure is lonely, though."

"Well, that's a musician's life on the road, right? Maybe you should use that loneliness to inspire a new song."

"If that were the only problem, that would be swell."

The voice sounded genuinely perplexed. "What else could be the matter, Rusty?"

"Those cravings are starting to come back. And the steaks you gave me are starting to run out."

Silence.

"You still there?"

"Don't worry, Rusty. I have someone on the way to you. Can't let you go all rogue biter now that you're a TV star, can we?"

"No, I don't believe that would be ideal."

"Rest up, Rusty! We'll talk soon." And with that, Rusty's only friend was gone.

As he sat on the edge of his hotel room bed, fear started to take over. He knew not what to do. A shower might cause more decomposition and he could go to sleep, but who's to say if the death that he managed to sidestep were to take him now? He was weary, and all sorts of emotions he hadn't felt since the old days. But that was before the experiment. That was during the dark times, when God had indeed kicked him out of Heaven, or at least that was what the nice Spanish fella had said. It hadn't given him his facilities back. The kind man on the phone had. The story and subsequent first song that detailed how Rusty had been sent back from Heaven? Well, the guidance of the Spanish-fella had done it again. Him and his friends who didn't speak much and had rather fearsome looking teeth.

Like any being that's exhausted from work and worry, Rusty eventually fell asleep. But not before he cried some confused tears and noodled on the guitar a little. Final death would not take Rusty, even though his demise would have solved several problems.

* * *

THE FIRST EPISODE of the third season of *America's Next Country Star* started off with six contestants, including Rusty. Unfortunately, poor Penelope Winston's voice cracked during her attempt to cover Dolly Parton's *Jolene.* America noticed and voted her off that night. Everyone else, including Rusty, sang like an angel and therefore granted a stay.

Despite coming in second on the first round, Rusty and his pitch-perfect cover of Johnny Cash's *Folsom Prison,* was considered a novelty act by everyone on the show's staff outside of Miriam Hatfield. And like any novelty act, he wasn't expected to win. Maybe come in third, which as far as the producers were concerned, would be great in terms of diversity optics, but that was it.

While they were allowed to cover whatever song they wished in the first contestant challenge, they had to cover Kenny Rogers' songs for the second round. To make it interesting, each singer had to pick the song they would perform randomly from slips of paper in a cowboy hat prior to the actual taping. Then the show started with all its usual lights and flare as Debra Robin, an eighteen-year-old phenom from Dallas, sang her version of *But You Know I Love You*. The judges lamented that she sounded great, but she didn't make the song her own.

"Young lady, we love you, but you're not going to win coming out here being intimidated by Kenny Rogers. In fact, you probably had to Google him.

... so what're you scared for!" Will Ryder chided the girl only to find himself booed by the audience for being too hard on the cute teenager.

Performing *The Gambler* and *Lady* respectively, contestants two and three did well enough to escape with more compliments than scolding. Then there was contestant four, Greg Price, who noticeably missed several notes during his rendition of Rogers' *Just Dropped in To See What Condition My Condition Was In.*

No surprise to anyone who understood how TV producers think that Rusty had been slated to perform last. They knew viewers would stay tuned to see the 'novelty act'.

It was a vocal tour de force, born from the fact that he was lucky enough to pull the one Roger's song that was experiencing a sort of rebirth among young people who weren't even born when the country music legend dropped *Ruby Don't Take Your Love to Town*.

When he finished, the entire theater was on its feet for the longest standing ovation in the show's history. Miriam Hatfield was openly weeping, completely overcome with emotion. Then things quieted down as Harpy joined him onstage, "Okay, Rusty! Now, let's see what the judges have to say about that."

From the judge's table, Chet ruled on Rusty's performance first. "Rusty, I must ask. Are you sure you're not Kenny Rogers come back to life?"

If he were not of undead green pallor, he might have blushed as he spoke into the microphone Harpy held up to his face. "No sir, Mr. Chet. I'm just old Rusty."

"It was wonderful! You have touched me down in my heart! God bless you, Rusty C. Nail," was all Miriam could manage between sobs.

"I think the world of you, too, Ms. Hatfield," Rusty said with a wry smirk. Fans of the show would see the question, 'Was zombie contestant flirting with Miriam Hatfield?' posted by bloggers all over social media within minutes of this interaction.

Meanwhile, Harpy's eyes were also filled with tears, but that was due to Rusty's smell, not his vocal stylings.

Even Will Ryder, the consummate skeptic, and the judge most expected to be cruel to Rusty no matter what, conceded. "I must admit, that was amazing, Rusty. I am deeply impressed."

The crowd erupted as Harpy threw to commercial break. "Well, now is the time for America to decide! Rustle up your phones and text your picks to 888-8888! When we return, we'll see which one of these singing sensations scored the highest and who will have to pack their things and ride off into the sunset! We'll be right back."

* * *

"I DON'T KNOW how to say this, but I don't think we should do this," Stephen Buja called out over his shoulder.

"We have no choice." Christian Brookwater's voice was filled to the brim with agitation. "We have to do this now."

Stephen Buja, a recently made vampire who had only months ago been appointed to serve as the vampire nation's Secretary of Technology and Education had planned to spend his evening updating protocols and restrictions to keep humans out of vampire internet servers. Then someone put a zombie on television and his whole schedule got rearranged. Now he was sitting at his desk watching *America's Next Country Star* on his laptop, waiting for a cue to disrupt the show's contestant voting. Meanwhile, the Lord of Vampires stood scowling two feet behind him.

Stephen was a mere human trying to protect a childhood friend who had become a werewolf when he first met the vampire that would one day rule over the entire *homo monstrous* community. The threesome would experience some terrifying adventures and form an alliance that would lead to a global truce between the previously warring vampire and werewolf factions.

Having worked for Christian for a while now, Stephen knew better than to contradict the moody vamp without a damn good reason. But in this moment, he felt Christian was making a big mistake.

"Chris... I mean Lord Brookwater..."

"Speak your piece, Stephen!"

"I don't know if you noticed this, but your zombie killed that song! I mean, I don't even like country music, and I thought he was amazing!"

Christian shook his head. "I realize it was a great performance. But this has got to happen ! I've got no other window!'

"But to say the votes would put him in last place after that? Someone is sure to launch an investigation!"

"An investigation I am trusting you to block," Christian snapped. "Now pull the trigger! Last place! He won't get eliminated otherwise."

Damn this sucks! Stephen thought as he turned back to his computer and began punching in codes. "All right, dammit! Give me one second!"

"And I suggest you be careful talking to me with all that bass in your voice!"

"Meant no disrespect, sire!"

"Fine, Stephen. Just do it."

A few more taps on the keyboard and it was over. Stephen slumped back in his chair as Christian pulled a cell phone from his leather jacket. "Helen! Standby! They should be sending him to his dressing room soon. Is that Gilbert guy there?"

"He sure is," Helen Reese, Christian's second in command, answered.

"Good! Remember what I said!"

Helen's British accent always intensified when she felt micromanaged. "Of course!"

Christian ended the call and leaned towards Stephen and patted him on the back. "Don't worry, kid. I have some ideas for how we can help the dead man country boy. But first, I gotta think big picture and get him the fuck off the TV."

Stephen nodded. "I get it. I just feel bad for him. I mean, he won the round. He soundly kicked their asses. People dream about shit like this."

The two vampires fell silent as the last commercial in the

break faded to black and their manipulation, for better or worse, would play out for the world to see.

* * *

WHILE BRAD and Harpy were no fans of how Rusty smelled, their discomfort from being around the undead singer was nothing compared to how they felt after their talk with the statistics team.

Brad shook his head, his lips curled in disgust. “They brought him in last. How the fuck did that happen? He was great. I mean, maybe third because he looks like hell, but Jesus!”

Staring into the stats guy’s laptop, Harpy looked ready to cry. “And I’m the one that has to get on national TV and announce this. I swear, I hate this fucking business!”

One stage manager called for Harpy to get on her mark while another helped guide the contestants to where they were supposed to stand. Make-up artists flurried to give everyone except Rusty touch ups. The first and last time one of the show’s make-up artists touched Rusty, a significant part of his left cheek peeled off. After that, Brad issued orders that the only cosmetic assistance Rusty would receive would be generous spray downs of air freshener.

“Thirty-seconds to live,” the lead stage manager shouted.

By now Brad had made his way to the judges’ table to brief them. When told the news, Miriam’s pallor turned almost as bad as Rusty’s.

“5…4…3…applause please!”

In homes across the United States, the opening animation rolled across TV screens, followed by a sweeping wide shot of the cheering crowd and the stage. The crowd settled and the robbery began.

Harpy was professional enough to attempt to hide what she

was truly feeling, but even passing acquaintances would remark on how she appeared visibly disturbed. "Welcome back to *America's Next Country Star*! All right, America, over the break the votes were tallied. You guys made some interesting decisions, that's for sure. And for the first time in the history of the show, the audience at home went in a completely opposite direction of the judges. Turns out tonight's front runner is none other than..." She paused for timpani drumroll and cymbal crash. "Debra Robin!"

At the announcement, a small blast of confetti shot into the air above Debra and lights flashed. At home, viewers watched a camera shot of all the contestants zoom in on the happy, but also visibly surprised young lady.

Harpy took a deep breath. "And now, we are going to show America the rest of the results."

The audience went from being happy for Debra to stunned silence as they saw the final tally in overhead monitors. "This means Jan and Paul are safe. And unfortunately, that means Rusty C. Nail from Coosa County, you will not be advancing."

Booing and confused muttering began to fill the air.

Miriam shot straight up in her seat. "I want to say something!"

"Well, yes Miriam, it is customary for the judges to send off the eliminated. What would you like to say?"

Miriam fought back tears as the theater fell silent. "It's a travesty. Here stands a man, brought back to us by the wisdom of Heaven. An unorthodox angel with a voice to match. And because of his appearance, he is deprived of his rightful place on that board. I mean no disrespect to you, Debra. In fact, I'm happy for you, sweetheart. But Rusty C. Nail is one of the best we have ever had on this show, and it just breaks my heart that he stands here, living proof of God's mercy, and he loses his place because, of all things, racism. We have to do better, America!"

For the outpouring, Miriam received a standing ovation as she sat down.

Then it was Chet's turn. "I'm not sure what happened, maybe we were preempted by some war stuff, who knows! But I'm sorry you're not making it. You have a great voice and I'm going to implore you to keep sharing your gift!"

This time the applause, while strong, was nowhere near as raucous as what Miriam received. When it settled, all eyes settled on Will Ryder.

"Look here folks! No one knows more than me about the history of the marginalized breaking into country music. Now, I'm still not sure I buy certain aspects of this whole thing, but one thing I was convinced of is things happen for a reason. And I think Rusty's apparent return from the grave only means he's supposed to be on this stage! And I'm glad he lost tonight, because I'm going to ask you, Rusty, to let me sign you to my damn label!" The crowd sprang to their feet, screaming with joy at Will's fixing what they clearly viewed as an injustice.

In her mind, Harpy was screaming a 'thank you' to Will as she ran over to Rusty and shoved her microphone in his face. "All right, Rusty! Big question! Are you going to sign?"

Rusty almost seemed to smirk. "Well, I'd be honored! With Mr. Ryder's tutelage I am sure we can come up with some hits for the country music world!"

More applause. Meanwhile, outside the theater, bloggers and celebrity gossip websites would have another take. *Did America's Next Country Star just pull a hoax to get the zombie contestant in the studio sooner?*

"Speaking of hits, Rusty, there's one last thing. Like all of our contestants, when you auditioned you had an original song. Since you're exiting and moving on to bigger things, why don't you play that little diddy that explains how you got here?"

"Well, don't mind if I do, Harpy!"

She turned to the camera as Rusty walked to center stage. "Ladies and gentlemen, giving us a taste of what country music fans will be clamoring for in the future, give it up for Alabama's own, Rusty C. Nail, singing 'Dead Man Country'."

As Harpy and the other contestants cleared out, the cameras found Rusty sitting on a stool. The stage lighting changed from television white to an intimate purple as a zombie with a slowly decomposing face and gifted voice once again told the story of his exit from heaven. And for those few minutes no one worried about whether the story was the truth or not, they only basked in the sheer beauty of what they were hearing and witnessing.

* * *

"SIGNED TO HIS LABEL?" Stephen Buja shouted.

Christian threw his head back. "Fuck me!" His glowing red eyes glued to Stephen's laptop screen and his fangs were extended from being irritated.

"You still going through with the extraction? I mean, look at him. Maybe we can think of another way?"

"There is no other way." Christian shook his head. "Go to Zoom!"

"But the song isn't ov..."

"I want to talk to Helen!"

"Okay, okay!" Stephen obliged the vampire lord and opened a second laptop.

"Honey! You there?" Stephen asked after a couple of taps on the keyboard.

The screen was black, but she heard him clearly enough. "Could you not call me that when I'm conducting official business?"

"Yes, buttercup!"

"She is going to fuck you up!" Christian tried to caution his lovesick techie before getting to business. "Helen, where are you?"

"I used my powers of persuasion to get hired on the theater security team. Just outside Rusty's dressing room. Earlier, I witnessed a rather unimpressive looking fellow sneaking inside. Since he hasn't come out, I can only assume it's that Gilbert bloke."

Christian nodded. At least something was going the way it was supposed to. "That's good."

"By the way, I'm glad you decided not to kill the zombie. He's very talented."

Christian rolled his eyes. "Yes, I know!"

"Anyway, I'm standing by," Helen said.

"Why is your screen black?" Stephen asked.

"Because I'm undercover. The phone is in my pocket, silly."

"Breast or butt?"

"Such a juvenile!"

"Enough! Both of you!" Christian snapped. "Helen, remember the plan?"

"Absolutely."

"Okay, standby. I think the song's almost over."

* * *

"WELL, that may be the last we see of the singing zombie on *America's Next Country Star,* but it's not the last America will see of Rusty C. Nail, I can guarantee. From the Colgate Amphitheater in Memphis, Tennessee, we're wishing you a grand good night!"

The cheering continued well after the show faded to black and the stage manager's voice came over the public address system.

The audience loaded out as everyone on stage outside of

Rusty began making their way backstage. A few people made their way to Rusty and congratulated him on the contract, but for the most part, the scene onstage felt just like the hotel bar party: very cliquish.

Despite the applause, the accolades, and the promise of a recording contract, Rusty couldn't help but feel a little angry. There was something else. He was hungry and not for the turkey and avocado wraps in his dressing room.

I need to get off this stage before I hurt someone.

He didn't know where his guitar case was and didn't care. Normally the type of guy who saunters, Rusty was full on speed-walking, trying to exit stage left.

Will, who had stopped to sign autographs for fans who'd all but rushed the stage at the end of the show, happened to spot Rusty's hasty exit. "Rusty! My agent will call you tomorrow and we'll set things up, okay?"

Rusty barely glanced back. "Whatever you say, sir!"

Once off the stage, he marched down the corridor to his dressing room, which incidentally was isolated from everyone else's dressing rooms, the green rooms, the press junket area, the control room and pretty much everything else. Normally reserved for high-end divas, Brad decided the room's location in the theater made it the best place to put the odorous Rusty.

As Rusty stepped to the door and reached for the knob. A woman's hand grabbed his wrist. "Not so fast, Mr. Nail."

Rusty turned to face what appeared to be an attractive, red-headed British lady dressed in all black. "Ma'am?" Something about her didn't feel right. "Wait a..."

She clamped her left hand over Rusty's mouth and pulled her Glock with the other. "Shh!"

He obeyed as she opened the door, turned, and walked into the room where she immediately found herself face to face with another man holding a gun.

"What the hell?"

"You Gilbert?"

"Why do you have a gun, Gilbert? Your orders were to capture this zombie, not kill him. Considering he was just on TV, I would say he's pretty docile, wouldn't you? You could have done that with a taser."

"Says who? Who are you?"

"I'm from upper management!"

Gilbert's eyes grew wide with fright. "Wait! You're a…"

"Don't get your knickers in a twist, love." Helen turned to pull Rusty into the dressing room. "Just know that if you shoot this zombie, I'm authorized to drink every drop of blood in your body."

As Gilbert lowered his weapon, an incredulous Rusty turned to Helen. "I knew something was wrong with you! You're…"

"British. Yeah, I know." She pulled her phone out of her jacket. "Christian, you still there?"

"Gotcha loud and clear," the vampire lord answered. "Hold me up to Gilbert first."

She did as she'd been instructed. "Hello! Do you know who I am?"

Gilbert might have pissed himself. "Oh my God! Are you Christian Brookwater?"

"Exactly. Now I just have one question for you. Were you going to shoot that zombie?"

Gilbert's voice quaked. "Yes, but only because that is what Raymond told me to do."

Christian nodded. "Okay, kid. Here is the deal. You're going to leave the gun somewhere in that room and you are going to go home. Do you understand me?"

"Yes, sir!"

Gilbert put the gun down on a small table next to the turkey wraps and with one last look at Rusty, as he made for the door. "You were great tonight, by the way."

"Very kind of you to say, sir," Rusty said as he tipped his hat.

Once Gilbert was gone, Christian's voice rang out of the phone. "I think he pissed himself."

"He totally pissed himself," Helen affirmed as she turned the phone towards herself. "Would you like to speak to Mr. Nail now?"

"Yes, please."

Rusty's eyes filled with curiosity as Helen repositioned the phone so they could see each other. "Christian? The vampire lord? They told me I was supposed to write a song about you once I was famous."

"Speaking of that, do you have a name you could provide?" Christian asked.

"You want the names of the vampires that did this to me? I never knew their names, sir. I didn't know anyone by name except Raymond. They kind of made him be my handler, in a manner of speaking. Once they'd put whatever drug they'd shot into me to make me like this, all alert and not hungry, whatever they wanted, they just told him."

"What was all that business about how you got kicked out of heaven?"

Rusty shrugged. "It's just a song, sir. I had no idea it would get people riled up, least of all Miriam Hatfield."

Christian chuckled. "Okay look, I want to get you back to my compound and let my people run some tests on you. Nothing crazy or invasive. Nothing that should hurt too bad. I just want to find out how they did this to you. Now, if you could just go along with the lady I sent to rescue you, I would appreciate it."

Rusty looked as if he were considering his options and finally realizing he had none. "I suppose you're going to be putting a stop to my record deal situation?"

Christian sighed. "Rusty, I swear, I'll make it up to you somehow."

Kill Kill Kill

"All right then."

"Thank you, Rusty. Trust me, you're doing the right thing."

"You're welcome."

"Helen?"

"Yes, Christian?

"Slight change on the order. Forget about leaving the corpse."

Helen's eyes narrowed. "Really? That was the most expensive part of the trip."

"Dump the body and come home."

"As you wish."

The call ended.

* * *

BACK IN NEW YORK, Stephen turned to Christian. "What are you going to do now?"

"Well, first I am going to get Raymond and interrogate him."

"You gonna kill him after?"

Christian shook his head. "I met Raymond when he was twelve. His grandmother's last words were to me, for me to take care of him. Despite this betrayal, he's like family to me. I'm not going to kill him. I may beat the snot out of him and imprison him for the rest of his life, but I can't kill him."

"What if he doesn't give you the names of the vampires that created Rusty?"

Christian's eyes turned their deepest red. "Oh! That I'm not worried about."

Stephen said a quiet prayer for Raymond as he watched Christian exit through the door.

* * *

THE SUDDEN DISAPPEARANCE of Rusty C. Nail sent shockwaves through the *America's Next Country Star* fanbase and birthed conspiracy theories that would live on for years. When reached for comment Will Ryder had an interesting theory. "Maybe the good Lord, in his infinite wisdom, decided to take Rusty back unto his bosom." An inconsolable Miriam Hatfield would join Will in presenting that as Rusty's final chapter.

The night after Rusty's disappearance, Christian read Will's remarks off a computer screen in his office when he was summoned to the loading dock World Vampire Council's main office building. He was greeted by several of his soldiers and Helen. At Helen's side sat a hospital gurney.

"What happened?" he asked.

Helen pulled the blanket away, revealing Rusty triple-strapped to his gurney. Sadly, his eyes were blank like any other ghoul's. At the sight of Helen's face, Rusty hissed and struggled against his restraints. Spittle ran down his face.

"He turned back to being a regular zombie while we were bringing him in," Helen explained.

Christian punched the air. "Damn!"

Helen pulled her Glock from its holster. "Should I put him out of his misery?"

"No! Raymond is here. I'm going to make him tell me what he knows. Then we are going to restore Rusty, just as he was."

Even without the British accent, Helen's tone dripped with sarcasm. "Because the world needs a country singer zombie?"

"Because the world could use whatever makes zombies cognizant and I need to behead the people who did this to embarrass me. It's a win, win."

"You can admit you like the song; you know?" Helen mocked.

"Shut up!" Christian said as he walked away.

Before giving the order for the other vampires to take Rusty to the lab, she looked down in his angry face one last time. Somewhere behind those ravager's eyes was a fantastic musician. And she agreed with Christian that there was nothing wrong with saving him.

The End

FROM WITHIN THE HULL

MARC ABBOTT

The ship appeared as a dark silhouette against the light of the full moon. Its long shadow rippled atop the surface of the water as a slight breeze picked up. Her sails were down, making her masts more pronounced. No lanterns burned. No voices stirred. No life at all moved atop the deck. The faint cry from creaking wood was all that echoed in the night. For all anyone knew, she was derelict at sea.

That was Captain Hawkins' first thought as his slave ship sailed slowly past a massive, four-mast cargo ship whose shadow seemed to swallow them. It was difficult to tell her colors in the night, so he wasn't sure if she was a British ship or American. But there was something eerie about the situation. Despite being on warm waters, a chill cut through him. He took a swig from the bottle of rum, clutched it tight then scratched his stubble with his thumb.

"This is damned peculiar," he mumbled.

The watch stander rang the bell. Captain Hawkins, a burly man with an unkept beard, dressed in knee-high boots, close-fitting breeches with a form-fitting shirt, moved quickly to him, seized his wrist, and spoke through clenched teeth just above a whisper.

"Don't." He tipped his head at the ship. "We pass quietly."

"What's wrong, Captain?" the watch stander said with a look of concern.

"Something doesn't feel right. That ship's too still."

"She looks abandoned."

"Yeah? When was the last time you saw an abandoned ship with her sails down?" Captain Hawkins pointed up to her mast.

"You think it's pirates? Ambush maybe?"

"Tell the helmsmen to stay this course. Don't deviate. Let the wind take us past."

The Captain looked up at his sail and watched the breeze continue to do its duty and push them ahead. He summoned one of the cabin boys, a 13-year-old named Corbin, who was on deck getting air.

"Yes, captain?"

"Corbin, go forward and see if you see a name on the side of this ship," he said. "As soon as you do, report back to me. Don't yell it out, but hurry back the moment you see anything."

"Yes, captain," Corbin said. He ran to the forward, lit a lantern, and held it up and out over the side of the ship to see.

Captain Hawkins took another swig and then moved to the third mate, Andrew Woodland.

"Mister Woodland, gather some men, arm yourself, and secure the hull. If this is an ambush, we need to protect our cargo." Before Andrew could answer, Captain Hawkins drew his pistol and put the barrel under his chin. "And if it is, they'd better not breach us, or I'll personally send you to the land of the dead. And you know I mean it."

Andrew swallowed hard as he rolled his eyes down to peer at Captain Hawkins' hand and nodded quickly. As the pistol lowered, Andrew moved away quickly and gathered a group of crewmen then led them to the stairs going to the hull.

Captain Hawkins started to follow, keeping his eye on the ship. They were close to clearing it when Corbin came running to him.

"Captain, I saw her name, sir. It's the *Adroa*."

"*The Adroa*?" He tried to recall the name. He looked aft for his second mate. "Mister Bristol, come here."

Elliot Bristol, a wary-looking man with a disheveled look, came to him. "Sir?"

"Do you know of a ship called the *Adroa*?"

"Is that the name of this one we're sailing by?"

"It is."

Elliot turned to it. "Neither the name nor the look of that ship is familiar to me." He turned back to Captain Hawkins. "She could be a new ship."

"That's possible. Or she could be stolen and the name changed?"

"Pirates don't usually put the names of their ships on display. They let the jolly roger do the talking, though I don't see a flag up there."

"Will you arm the rest of the men, and keep them armed, until we are well past this thing?"

"Captain?" Corbin tapped him.

"What?"

"Look." Corbin pointed.

Captain Hawkins looked up at the deck of the *Adroa*. From stern to forward, lined up perfectly, were the dark silhouettes of men. In a cascade of lantern light along the rail, their faces began to glow. The ship slowly started to dip into the sea until they were all at eye level. He could now see their faces and upper bodies. Their eyes were cloudy white. Their upper torso skin looked devoid of pigmentation. Several of them wore metal collars around their necks. A clear indication they were slaves. They appeared to be in a trance. Then, in unison, they started to chant the name *Ogbundabali*. They raised their hands, exposing an array of machetes and knives. As the *Adroa* drifted closer to them, Elliot pointed to a particular man among the slaves. A white man aimed his blade at them.

"Captain, that's. . . Dear God, that's John Brown. But he's dead."

* * *

FIFTY SLAVES STOOD on the deck of the *Margaret* in a tight group. Chains rattled at their wrists and feet as they watched twenty more of them brought up from the hull. The crew, armed with clubs and machetes, had flanked them, preparing to fight in case the slaves tried to revolt. When the twenty men had joined the fifty, Captain Hawkins called out to his second mate, John Brown.

"Mister Brown, move these slaves to the stern. Mister Bristol and Mister Woodland, see that the crew makes certain none of them step out of line. Any one of you so much as let one of these slaves make a move or do anything to cause any problems," he cocked his pistol, "you get a bullet in your head and tossed overboard. Now move it!"

Elliot grinned, drew his pistol, and took aim at the crew as well. The crewmen closed in around the slaves and began poking them with their weapons, ushering them to the back of the ship. The only sound made was that of their chains as they shuffled their feet. None of them made eye contact with the crew for fear it would set off a chain reaction of brutal beatings and cuts.

When they reached the stern, Captain Hawkins, standing at the wheel, pointed to a crate with a large iron ball in it as rope coiled atop it.

"Mister Brown, if you would, take the rope and tie it to the ankle of that slave." He pointed to a young black African who, judging from the look of terror on his face, had figured out what was about to happen. Captain Hawkins turned to a crewman holding a club. "You there, Foster, is it? Affix those chains so that these two groups are attached." He tossed him the keys to the shackles. "Now."

Foster placed the club down at the foot of the slave closest to him. The second he moved to unlock the shackle, a shot rang out. The back of Foster's head exploded, sending blood and brain matter onto the bodies of the slaves and the deck of the ship. He fell over atop his club, dead.

Everyone reacted with slaves backing up and crewmen putting distance between them. John Brown stopped working and stared in disbelief.

"Captain?"

"That moron put his club down at the foot of this slave. I warned him." He began reloading the pistol. "Mister Brown. Retrieve the key and affix those chains. Then finish with the rope." He pointed to another crewman. "You, Reeves, toss that body over the side. One less bastard I have to pay now."

John Brown took the key and did what he was told. When he was finished he went back to the rope and attached it. Then he tossed the key back to Captain Hawkins.

Captain Hawkins scratched his beard as he rolled his tongue against the inside of his bottom lip. He stopped long enough to watch Reeves lift and carry the dead one to the railing and toss him over. Before he could turn around, Elliot shot him in the back of the head, sending him into the sea.

"Why?" John asked.

"He moved too slow," Elliot said, fiendishly.

"Very good, Mister Bristol," Captain Hawkins said, nodding

in approval. "That's how you take charge of the situation. You'll be captain of your own ship at this rate."

"Thank you, Captain." He turned to Andrew, grinning widely. "You hear that? Me, a captain."

"We should all be lucky," Andrew mumbled.

"Now let that be a lesson to the rest of you," Captain Hawkins announced. "Pull your weight or suffer the consequences."

"Captain, I don't understand your actions against the slaves," John said.

"You questioning my orders, Mister Brown?"

"I am just trying to understand why we would throw precious cargo over the side of the ship, that is all."

Captain Hawkins didn't answer immediately. He turned his attention to the slaves. "It seems we're running a bit low on rations with four days left to port. At the rate we're sailing, we're going to ration even more, which means food is going to get scarce." He turned to John. "I did the numbers and if I pull into port with dead slaves, we don't get paid. But if we lost some of our cargo in transit, we can file a claim against the company and get our money that way."

"The company will never accept this, Captain. No one has ever won a claim for the loss of slaves. They will take it out of our pay regardless. And we already took on more hands for this trip for a bigger payday."

"Then I need to make sure we all get a substantial cut. So far, we've lost two crewmen trying to stop the slaves from going overboard." He cocked the pistol and haphazardly aimed it at the crewmen, and then at the slaves. "Probably lose a couple more tomorrow. Who knows?"

"Captain Hawkins, I protest," Andrew said.

"You protest?"

"Captain, you do this, and it sets a bad precedent. It will cost us work. Not only do we run the risk of not getting paid but who would hire us again if we can't bring in cargo unspoiled?" John said.

Andrew chimed. "Or just dump'em at sea?"

"Don't tell me you're concerned for the lives of these niggers."

"It's not so much about the slaves than it is about our reputation and our pay," John said.

"I see. And you believe I don't care about either?" Captain Hawkins slowly approached them.

"I didn't say that," John said.

"That's not what it sounds like to me," Elliot said.

"You shut up. No one is talking to you," John said. He turned to address Captain Hawkins and jumped when he saw that he was just steps away from his face.

"You know, for a second mate, you have a lot of mouth on you."

"You hired me to make sure the cargo was well looked after."

"I did not hire you. You are only *still* on this ship out of respect for her last captain whom you served. And the only reason he hired you was to keep the slaves in line since you're dark enough that they don't see you as a threat."

"I'm a white man."

"Ha, you're not a white man. I'm white; you're a mutt," Elliot said.

John lunged for Elliot. Before he could get hold of him, Captain Hawkins put the barrel of his pistol to the back of John's head. John froze.

"Better mind yourself. Put your hands on my first mate and I'll blow your head clean off, is that understood?"

John nodded. "All the way, Captain."

"And you, Mister Woodland?"

"Aye."

"Mister Brown, look at me." Captain Hawkins leaned his pistol back. John turned to him. "Don't concern yourself on how

I operate. Do what you're told. You do that and I might see my way to paying you a full wage. Is that clear?"

"It is, Captain."

"Well then," Captain Hawkins took his free hand and backhanded John hard across the face. "That's for mouthing off." He slapped him across the other side of his face. "Fuckin' move the slaves to the rail and throw the iron over the side. And as far as this matter is concerned, we lost them to sickness, is that understood?"

John rubbed the side of his face. He started to speak and was struck again. He could feel his anger building up as his hands shook. Rather than respond, he moved to the box, summoned a crewmember to help him, and together they lifted the ball and threw it overboard.

The rope made a zipping sound as it slid over the rail at high speed. The slaves began screaming and trying to run back toward the main deck. Several of them managed to get their hands on crewmembers, clutching their arms and wrists for dear life.

The slave with the rope around his ankle was pulled into the rail with so much force that he dislocated his hip. The loud snap was followed by his cries of agony as he went over the top, taking two more with him. The fourth slave grabbed for the edge of the rail, but the weight of the first three was too much and his hand slipped. One by one they all went over, taking two more crewmen with them as they plunged into the chilly Atlantic waters and were dragged to the black depths.

Captain Hawkins peered over the side to make sure they were all gone. After a moment he turned to John.

"At least you tied them properly. You do good work when you're focused, Mister Brown."

"There's a chance those crewmen will float back to the surface. They weren't tied. What if another ship finds them?"

Captain Hawkins chuckled. "And so what? They won't be alive if they are discovered. If they don't drown, sharks will get them. Now, Mister Woodland, go double-check the rations. Mister Brown, make sure we have enough water for the remaining slaves. I have to go put this in the log." He looked at Elliot. "Mister Bristol, get these men back to work."

He carefully put the hammer of the pistol back in place, tucked the weapon into his waist, and retired to his quarters. Elliot fired a shot into the air and the crew scurried back to their posts.

John and Andrew walked toward the hatch that led to the hull where the slaves were kept.

"You need to be careful," Andrew said above a whisper. "That man is a sadist. He'll kill you for breathin' loudly."

"I can handle myself. I'm more concerned about you. Elliot's behavior is garnishing favoritism with the captain. He's always been a bit unstable, but he's gotten worse since he had you demoted and took your spot."

"Yeah, I've noticed. How's your face?"

"I have to admit, that blow hurt." John winced as he touched where Captain Hawkins had struck him. "I had to struggle to keep from hitting him back."

"Thank God ya didn't. Look, I've sailed with a wicked slave ship captain before, but this man... spit right from the ninth level of hell he was. He got no compassion like Captain George. So, lemme give ya an extra word of advice. Be careful how you talk to him 'bout the slaves. To him, you sound like you feel somethin' for them. You gotta remember they are just cargo."

"Precious cargo, and I can't help but feel something for them. Human or materials doesn't matter. Any damage to them, we pay for it. Know what happens when a captain doesn't pay his crew? Things get ugly fast. The last thing I want to end up being is a crewman on the Flying Dutchman," John said.

"Too much talking, more work," Elliot said as he walked up behind them. "Slave lovers."

Andrew turned, his hand balled into a fist, ready to strike. Elliot raised his pistol and aimed at Andrew's head.

"Put that down," John commanded.

"Or what?" Elliot said.

John reached for the pistol and Elliot turned it on him and pulled the hammer back. "Are you crazy?"

"Give me a reason, mutt."

John turned and walked away. "Go ahead. Only cowards shoot a man in the back."

Andrew laughed. Elliot turned and fired a shot alongside his face. Andrew screamed and fell to his knees covering his ear. A trickle of blood ran down his neck.

John rushed back to his side to check on him as Elliot chuckled and walked away.

"Let me see. How bad is it?"

"I'm okay. Go tend to the slaves." Andrew looked at him. "Watch your back."

John stood, helped Andrew to his feet, and watched him walk away. He then looked at Elliot, who stared at him with an evil glare.

"Go be with your kind down there," he said.

John opened the hatch, then stood at the top of the steps and stared down at the hull. The smell, a mixture of sweat and human excrement, made him gag. He could see the barrel of water used to keep the slaves from going thirsty just off to the right. However, he couldn't tell from his angle how much was in there. He covered his nose and mouth with his hands, then began his slow descent.

He thought about Elliot's remarks, calling him a mutt. He wasn't far off. He was the product of an interracial affair between his father and a woman who had been an indentured servant in the house they lived in among other working sailors. He had never met the woman because his father's wife had the landlady dismiss his birth mother dismiss her from the home shortly after he was born. And because she herself couldn't bear children; she claimed him as her own. But as soon as his skin started to brown, she left them and was never seen again.

When he was old enough, he worked with his father on merchant ships. No one knew they were father and son; they just assumed John was his father's servant. He worked as a cabin boy until he was old enough to work on the deck.

When it came to his encounters with slaves, while loading them onto the ship, he noticed they weren't as scared of him as they were of the white crew members. They would try to talk to him in their language when they didn't think other crewmen were near and they would listen to him when he was given the task of gathering them on deck. He would even slip them extra food from time to time because as long as they stayed calm and complacent, the chances of them uprising were slim. The captains of the various ships he crewed noticed his effect on slaves and often put him in charge of them. This often drew outrage from the more sadistic individuals who wanted to oversee them and felt John, even with a little blackness in him, was too black to be in charge. They complained, but between stories of slave revolts and mutinies, the captains felt it best to let John do what he does. He knew how to handle himself.

Captain Hawkins needed him. That was a fact, and no one, not even Elliot, would convince him otherwise.

He was halfway to the hull when he stopped, closed his eyes, and cleared his mind of the captain and his first mate. The slaves would know some act of violence had been perpetrated against their brothers and be on edge.

The hull was dim. Some cracks from between the wood of the deck above cast streams of light that crossed several of the slave's bodies and faces. John could make out the silhouettes of the Africans chained together, sitting in groups in the middle and along the wall. He could feel their eyes on him, but they said nothing. As he stepped into the center, they all collectively started to back away from him. He could sense their apprehension.

"I'm checking the water. No one else is coming to take any more of you away."

They murmured amongst one another in their native language. Despite being around slaves for several years, John hadn't been able to understand the many different tongues and dialects spoken. He could sometimes figure out what they were saying through gestures, or if they used one word over and over. But he didn't understand everything fully.

They settled down but still kept a wary eye on him as he approached the barrel, picked up a cup that sat on a small shelf above, and reached inside. He didn't feel water touch the cup until he was near the bottom.

"That's not good," he said.

He heard the collective shaking of chains over the creaks and moans of the ship passing over the waves. He looked up and several slaves were standing facing him. One tall and muscular slave, whom the captain had nicknamed Goliath, stepped forward, leaned toward John, and looked as though he were trying to examine his face. It made him uncomfortable.

"Back away from me," John demanded. "All of you, sit back down. I'll get you some water soon."

Goliath inched closer. John took a step toward him and into a stream of light which highlighted the black and blueness of the swelling where he was struck. The slave pointed to it, turned to the others, and spoke in a language John didn't understand. The others began to talk among themselves. When Goliath held up his chains and then pointed to John, they all seemed to understand what he meant.

They began chanting one word; *Ogbundabali*. It started as a deep, resonating type of growl then gradually got louder until it was a rhythmic holler. They began to stomp their feet and raise their hands to the ceiling.

"Stop that." John put the cup back. "Stop it before I have to take a whip to you."

They took a step closer to him and froze. John could see the red in their eyes as they fixed their gaze on him. It chilled him. Goliath pointed at him and then at the wall. He repeated the word and they began to chant. John tried to guess what they were saying to him.

"Are you trying to curse me? Stop it!" John snatched up the cup and, gripping it tightly, leaned over and swung it at Goliath's head, striking him so hard he fell over. The others around him rushed to his aid. John started to feel nervous. Not by the slaves but by the thought of what Captain Hawkins would do to him if he damaged any of them. Especially one as fit as Goliath. He leaned in and saw there was a gash on the side of their head. He got closer. The other slaves gave him room. He sat the slave up, and their eyes met. The slave looked woozy.

"Don't you black out on me," John said. "I'm sorry I struck you, but I warned you to stop."

"What did you do?" the voice of Captain Hawkins called from behind.

John looked back and there was Elliot with the captain.

"Told you I heard a commotion," Elliot said.

"Mister Brown, I sent you down there to report on the water rations, and Mister Bristol tells me that he heard chanting from the hull. Then I find you apologizing to slaves?" Captain Hawkins said. "What the hell are you up to?"

"I had to deal with an unruly one. That's all, captain."

"You had better not spoiled him."

"I had to strike him but he's alive. Just a bruise."

"Just a bruise." Captain Hawkins was on him in just a few strides and back handed John on the other side of his face. "Like that?"

John did his best to shake it off. "It's not like I whipped him."

"No, just apologize to him like he were a fellow crewman," Captain Hawkins said.

"You sure you weren't down there getting them riled up to try and take this ship and put yourself as captain?" Elliot said.

"I'm not that ambitious," John chided.

"Storm! Storm ahead!" the helmsman called out to him from the stern.

Captain Hawkins, Elliot, and John rushed back to the deck and looked forward. A mile-long, dark gray storm cloud had formed. Lightning danced within as thunder rolled. A thick shower of rain fell into the sea over violent waves.

"There's no way around," Captain Hawkins assessed. "Better get the men to their stations. We'll go through it."

"Sir, this might be a good time to clean the slaves," Elliot interjected. "Put them on deck in the storm and let the rain wash the filth and stink off them."

"That's an excellent idea. Mister Brown, go and get the slaves up here. Chain them to. . . Mister Brown?"

John didn't respond. He stared into the storm as though he were in a trance. At the entrance of the storm, he spotted what looked to be a large ship being jostled. It appeared to be turning away from them and going into the rain.

"You see that? That looks like a ship."

"Mister Brown, are you listening to me?"

"Captain, I thought I saw. . . ."

"I don't care what you think you saw."

"What if it's pirates? Perhaps you're not aware of what happened to the *Elizabeth Vane*?"

"I am." Elliot chimed in. "She was the slave ship that was beset upon by a band of pirates and then set ablaze. They say many of the crew were captured and killed."

"It wasn't just pirates. It's believed the ship was manned by escaped slaves as well. And the crew wasn't just killed, they were tortured. They hung the captain from the yard arm til he was nearly dead, then they dropped him in shark-infested waters. You want to run into that ship?" John said.

"I know how to defend my ship and when the time comes, you better be up for the challenge. Now, bring the slaves up and secure them properly. And keep a special watch on that one you injured. Because, Mister Brown, when we clear this storm, I find one slave missing, I'll personally flog you. Now go!"

John watched as the captain made his way to the helm. He glanced back at the storm to see if he saw the ship again. There was no sign of it. He called Andrew and two deckhands to assist him. They went back into the hull where they found all the slaves sitting up. They had managed to turn their bodies in the direction of the ship's forward and were chanting.

"What's got them riled up?" Andrew asked.

John looked in the direction of Goliath. He was the only one not facing forward, but was looking right at John, not saying a word.

"I don't like this," Andrew said. "It feels like they're planning something."

"I think they're praying," John said. "They do that from time to time."

"You think their God ever hears them?"

"I could care less," John said as he approached Goliath, knelt, and undid the chain from its base. "Doesn't have anything to do with me."

"We should silence them before we go up top."

"Let them be," John said. "Let them pray. If it keeps them complacent, that's all that matters." John stood and tugged on the chain. "Let's go."

Goliath stood. As he did, the ones behind him followed. John tossed the key to Andrew, who unlocked the chain from his end. He tossed the key back to John, tugged the chain, and the slaves slowly stood and began to converge on Andrew. He backed up, but the slaves continued to approach while chanting. The two deckhands advanced and started to struggle with the slaves.

"John!" Andrew screamed.

John turned, saw what was happening, and yelled for them to stop moving. When they didn't, he spoke one word, *Ogbundabali.*

The slaves stopped moving. They turned toward John and lined up.

"What did you say?" Andrew said.

"Never mind, it worked. Let's get up top." John pulled on the chain and led the slaves up to the main deck.

THE HELMSMAN FOUGHT with the wheel as the ship got knocked around in the storm. Waves struck the forward of the vessel, rose to breach the deck, and came crashing down atop the slaves as they sat chained together on the deck. The drag of the receding water nearly took several of them over the sides. They did their best to pull one another back from the brink by their chains as they were drenched in seawater.

John was knocked down and nearly tumbled down into the hull. He managed to catch himself on a rope that had come loose from the main mast just as the ship listed hard to starboard. That was when he heard a series of high-pitched screams coming from the slaves. He wiped the water from his face and looked in their direction.

Goliath and four others were on their backs, their legs in the air and bodies pressed against the rail. The chain connecting the ankle bracelets was over the side of the ship and in the sea. The one pressed hardest against the rail started to slide up over the side.

"No, no, no!" John let go of the rope and allowed himself to slide to them. He took hold of the slave about to go over just as the ship listed to the port side. He heard the crack of bone as the slave's foot bent forward from the chain pulling on the clamp. John managed to stand and take hold of the chain. He peered over the side and saw that it was still connected to another slave who was in the sea, struggling to stay above the surface despite his wrists still shackled.

John bent over, took hold of the chain, and tried to pull him up, but the weight and the slipperiness of the metal made it impossible for him to get a firm grip. Twice, he almost went over the side. He stood to wipe the water from his face. There was a flash of lightning and for a split second, he thought he saw the silhouette of the other ship moving alongside them in the storm. He froze and kept looking. Another lightning flash revealed it was keeping pace with them. A large dark vessel that listed with the sea. She had no lanterns lit and her presence sent an ominous feeling through him.

The slaves began chanting *Ogbunabali.* John saw they were all facing the vessel that traveled alongside them. Their arms raised to the dark, stormy skies.

Out of the corner of his eye, he saw the four slaves he had come to rescue stand. Goliath embraced them. They huddled together and as the ship listed again, he called out to the vessel, then they threw themselves over into the dark depths. John rushed to grab the tall one but was too late. He looked over the side and watched them disappear below the surface. He looked up at the ship. It was gone.

"What in the devil are you doing, Mister Brown?" The captain seized him by the arm. "What just happened?"

John looked at Captain Hawkins, speechless. Standing behind him were Elliot and Andrew, and several members of the crew. He turned back to where the ship had been and pointed. "I just saw that ship again. It was keeping pace with us, then slaves went overboard and . . ."

"You lost slaves to the sea?" He raged.

"It wasn't my fault."

"It will be the cat for you when we get out of this storm and whatever we lost will be deducted from your pay." The captain shoved him into the rail and then summoned the others to follow him as he made his way, stumbling, toward the stairs leading to the sitting slaves. "Get these slaves back in the hull, now!"

John watched as Elliot, Andrew, and the crewmen slipped and slid trying to get the slaves on their feet and back down into the bowels of the ship. He turned again to the storm just as lightning danced across the sky. The other ship was indeed gone.

* * *

THEY CAME out of the storm onto a calm, black sea. The sky was devoid of any clouds while the moon shone so bright, its reflection seemed to light up the water. Despite this, the crewmen lit several lanterns and placed them strategically on the deck so there was a ring of light in the center of the deck. They then gathered in a semi-circle at the edge of the ring and waited for the captain to arrive. Tied to the mast with his back exposed and the side of his face pressed against it, was John.

John could hear the footsteps of Captain Hawkins approaching. His sweat turned cold. He had only ever been whipped by his father and that was when he was a child. And a belt was far milder a punishment than a whip. But a whip was more humane than the cat of nine tails if you could say that being whipped was a humane act. He knew the damage it could do and no amount of anticipation of the first blow would prepare him for the tearing of his flesh.

Captain Hawkins stood before him gripping a cat of nine tails firmly. The tiny, spiked balls at the tips of the leather strands tapped against one another. Elliot stepped up alongside him.

"There were eight slaves on that chain you let go into the sea. So, it will be eight lashes for you." The captain waved the cat of nine tails before John's eyes. "I'll be doing the first four myself. Mister Bristol will finish the job. And then he will be my new first."

John gazed at Elliot, smirked then lowered his head. There was no use in protesting. He shut his eyes and prepared for the beating.

Captain Hawkins circled behind him, grunted, and within seconds, John felt the spikes from the cat slice the flesh of his back like claws. The searing pain caused John to see stars, and he let out a scream. He could feel blood seeping from the wounds and trickling down his back. Just as he was getting his vision back, he was struck across the opposite side of his back. The pain was intense with this blow. He felt dizzy. His body trembled. The next two blows came in succession, splitting the open wounds he already had more. He vomited. He started to feel weak like he wanted to sleep. But he fought to keep his eyes open.

On the next lash, one of the spikes dug into the wound and wouldn't come out. The captain tugged hard and the feeling of his flesh being ripped from his body caused John to black out.

He started to come to as he felt his body floating. He saw the night sky moving slowly above. Then, he felt what could only be fingers under his back, pressing into his wounds. He tilted his head to one side and saw that he was being carried by Andrew who gave him a sad look. He looked to the other side and there was another, and behind him was Elliot holding the bloody cat of nine tails. He then felt an iron clamp around his ankles.

"On you. Mister Bristol," the captain said.

"What?" John called out weakly.

"Throw him into the sea with the rest of the slaves," Elliot said.

The fingers below him shifted, then he felt himself being thrown backward. All he could see was the sky before his body struck the water. The salty sea ate at his wounds, stinging his back. He attempted to tread water but the combination of loss of blood, exhaustion from pain, and his legs in shackles made the struggle to break the surface futile.

He gave up before he had even tried. He held his breath as he slowly sank into the dark depths below. He looked down at the dark water, the silence that engulfed him was deafening. Maybe this was better. To not have to endure the cruelty of the ship, its captain, or the first mate. He wondered if this was the last thing the slaves who were cast at sea saw and felt. This was no way to die but maybe, in the grand scheme of things, death was better. But there was still a part of him that wanted to live. He released all the air from his lungs and ingested a large amount of seawater. He choked and convulsed as he began to drown. The life within him started to slip away. Just as the euphoric feeling of death started to overtake him, he saw what looked like a man swimming toward him out of the dark. He reached out to him just as his eyes closed.

* * *

John opened his eyes and found himself staring at a ceiling made of wood planks. It took him a moment to realize that he was in a room of some kind. He sat up on his elbows and saw that candles had been placed around him in a circle. It gave the room an ominous feel. He looked down at himself and saw that he was naked and covered in white powder. He tried to stand but his legs wouldn't allow it. That's when he heard movement to his left. He turned to look.

Just beyond the candles stood several men covered in the same powder. One by one, they took positions between the candles and stood stiff as boards while staring at him.

"Where am I?" he asked. They did not answer. "Hello? Can you tell me where I am?"

The men reached down in unison and picked up the candles. They took four steps back and the entire room seemed to brighten. Behind them stood an army of slaves and, scattered among them, some white men. All of them stared at him with eyes the color of storm clouds.

"You are aboard our ship, tha Adroa," a woman's voice said, though it wasn't in the room. Her voice was inside his head. It spoke in English but with a heavy African accent. He knew that from his time spent among slaves. *"You may stand, Slaver John."* He felt his legs start to move on their own, hoisting him into a standing position.

Once he was on his feet, the men holding the candles began to chant slowly .

"Who's talking to me?"

"Look in front of you."

He looked forward. There was a woman and a man, both wearing large headdresses adorned with multicolored feathers. They both held long ornate staffs, but it was the woman whose weathered face was painted white on one side. She took a step forward, examined his face then tapped the floor twice with the staff. Behind him, the army of slaves did the same with their feet.

"Where am I? Who are you?"

"We are Ogbundabali. God and Goddess of death," the man said in a booming voice.

"You are on tha ship of tha undead. You could say we are tha captain." She pointed the end of her staff at him. *"You are now part of this crew."*

"Ogbundabali? You're who the slaves have been calling to? You're real?"

"As you can see, we very much are."

"You saved my life."

"Your life was not mine to save."

"I commanded that your body be pulled from tha sea," the Ogbundabali man said.

"I kept your soul as payment."

"I don't understand."

The woman smiled. Her teeth were white like pearls. *"You are dead, Slaver John. How you died nota natural death but of one caused by evil. For that reason, I resurrected you back from tha dead as part of muh crew to exact revenge against tha evil that roams these watas. You are bound here, as part of tha living dead, until such time I see fit to release your soul to tha other side."*

John should have felt scared, but there was no emotion within him. Just a desire to ask, "What am I?"

"You are a zombie," said the Ogbundabali man.

He tried to move. "Why can't I move?"

"You have not been released, yet," the Ogbundabali man said. "I have will over your movements. You are free to move about tha ship but should you try to leave it or disobey an order you will be severely dealt with, Slaver John."

"I demand–"

The Ogbundabali man raised his staff and pointed it at him.

It felt as though all the air in the room had been sucked out. John's throat filled with water, which vomited from his mouth. He felt it in his nose next, making it impossible to breathe. "*But I'm supposed to be dead, how am I able to breathe?*" He tried to reach for his nose, but his arms wouldn't move.

"You breathe because I will you to breathe, Slaver John." The man's voice was louder and filled the room. "You are in a position to demand nothing. You belong to we and it is we who will decide when and what to tell you." He tapped his staff three times. "On your knees, Slaver!"

John fell to his knees. He felt as though he were drowning again and invisible chains were preventing him from using his arms and hands.

"Tha suffering you feel is due to your attachment to tha life you once had. That is the curse of being one of the undead. There is no real detachment from this life until body and soul are at rest."

The man banged his staff three times. John could breathe again. The sensation of water was gone. But he still had no control over his body.

"You will do our bidding." The Ogbundabali man moved closer. "Or, you will lay suffering, drowning for eternity." He tapped the staff three times again and John fell over.

"I will do your bidding."

"That wasn't a question or a choice, Slaver John ."

"Why do you keep calling me by that name?"

The woman pointed the head of the staff toward the opposite side of the room. He motioned to turn, and his legs allowed him to move. The slaves parted. Foster, Reeves, and the white crewmen dragged overboard from his ship stood before him. Their flesh had tuned a light blue hue. Their eyes were devoid of any signs of life. Alongside them were the slaves they had drowned along with Goliath, and those he had embraced before going overboard. They lumbered toward him, stopping only a few inches from the circle.

"These were your men and tha ones and your captain kept enslaved. Even though you cared for tha enslaved and are born of a woman who was treated as one, you are still guilty of participating in tha trade. But tha treatment against you was not warranted. For that, dey are prepared to accompany you."

"Accompany in what? What is it you want me to do then?"

"Our children call to us to be released from this world and live in tha next where dey are free. We answer their calls and prayers, rescuing them from their fate. You will lead tha zombie army into battle and free our children by destroying tha ships and tha evil men like tha one you served."

"Your participation in these crimes against our children in life means you must repent a thousand fold before any consideration can be given to allow you to cross over. It is our way," the Ogbundabali man said.

A stampede of footsteps from above interrupted them. The slaves all parted as a group of muscular zombified slaves rushed in. The one in the front held a machete. They knelt before Ogbundabali.

"Great Ogbundabali, the ship from the storm is approaching."

"Thank you, Borja," Ogbundabali said in unison. "Return to the deck and prepare for the attack."

The slaves rose, turned, and returned to the deck.

"Slaver John, it is time. Release our children, have the army kill all the crew, except one who will tell the tale of what they have seen. Then sink the vessel." Ogbundabali pointed to him with their staff. "You may kill the captain in the manner you see fit. We release you now, to do our bidding. Go kill the men who condemned you."

* * *

Captain Hawkins cocked the hammer back on his pistol and aimed at John. "I saw you drown! I don't know what manner of devilry this is, but I know you're dead." He fired a shot.

John felt something slap his shoulder. He looked over and saw there was a hole made by the bullet. He dug his finger into his dead flesh and pulled it out and let it fall into the sea. 1- He then leapt over the rail of the *Adroa* and landed on the deck of the *Margaret.*

"Dear God," Elliot said. "He's some kind of ghost."

Captain Hawkins reloaded his pistol quickly and fired again, hitting John in the chest. John began to lumber forward; in one hand he held a machete, in the other a cat of nine tails. It swung alongside him as he walked.

Captain Hawkins turned to Elliot. "Shoot him!" He started to reload again.

Elliot aimed with his pistol and fired. The bullet struck John in the head. John stopped walking. He lifted his machete to the sky and let out a terrifying groan. The zombies copied him and they began jumping onto the *Lilith.*

"Stand your ground, men!" Captain Hawkins cried out as one by one, the zombies attacked the crewmen. Striking with their knives and machetes. Turning the deck crimson with their blood.

A group of eight, led by Goliath, went after the helmsman. First butchering him with the blades then, using their bare hands, began to dismember his body. His cries of pain turned to gurgles and choking as he was killed.

Foster and Reeves went after Elliot, who dropped his pistol and tried to climb the main mast. They got hold of his legs and dragged him to the middle of the deck. He tried to fight them off but their grip was too strong. They pinned him down, Foster with his hands over his head and Reeves by his ankles. Borja straddled him and placed his hands on either side of his head and slowly started to crush it. Elliot cried out to God, but it did little to stay Borja's hand.

"Borja, no," John said in a gravelly voice. "Hang him."

Borja nodded, then seized Elliot by the throat. Foster and Reeves let him go and moved to the main mast and undid a rope. They fashioned it into a noose and waited as Borja lifted Elliot and brought him to them. They put the noose around his neck, tightened it, then released him. Borja looked at John, awaiting his command.

"From up there," John pointed up at the yardarm.

Borja pulled the rest of the rope off the mast and tied the end of it tight around his waist. He walked to a rope netting and began to climb up the mast to the yardarm. He fearlessly walked to the middle of it, stood straight then fell backward from it.

Elliot was violently jerked up into the air. His legs flailed while he grabbed at the rope around his neck. As Borja's body slammed onto the deck, the top of Elliot's head struck the yardarm. A spatter of blood exploded from his head as his body began to twitch and convulse. He then began to strangle in the noose.

John looked over at Borja as he lay unresponsive. He then looked around and summoned three zombies to go to him. As they moved to assist, Goliath, covered in the helmsman's blood, approached him.

"Go get your people from the hull and take them back to the ship. Stay there until we are done here."

Goliath slowly made his way to the hull. That's when John realized Captain Hawkins was no longer standing there. Instinctively, he sniffed the air. He could smell the spilled blood but there was another, more potent odor coming from the direction of the captain's quarters. Instead of following it, he turned to watch the zombie army attack the crew.

They broke off into smaller groups which enabled them to

catch more of the *Lilith* crewmen at one time. Not all of the zombies were using weapons. Many of them were choking the life out of crew members. One group beat two men to bloody pulps and then threw them over the side of the ship to drown. Another group got hold of the two deck hands that aided John in the hull and, using their hands, disemboweled them alive. The crack of a whip caught John's attention. He looked to his right and saw a zombie whipping a crewman who was being held by his arms by two other zombies. When he passed out he looked as though he were affixed to a cross. They then threw him overboard.

John spotted Corbin running frightened across the deck. The zombies weren't paying attention to him. He stopped close to a group that was stabbing a crewman to death, fell to his knees, and began to weep. John called the group to stop and seize Corbin. They did as ordered.

"Bring him." The zombies dragged Corbin to him. "I had forgotten about you."

"Mister Brown, sir, please."

John put the machete down and backhanded him across the face. As Corbin went limp, he picked up his machete. "Put him in that long boat over there."

As the zombies dragged Corbin to the longboat, John heard screaming from the opening that led to the hull. They weren't cries of joy for freedom. He looked and saw the newly released slaves rushing up from the hull, panic and fear on their faces as they seemed to be looking for an escape route. Several of them threw themselves over the side without a second thought. Others ran toward the *Adroa,* fell to their knees, and began to pray.

Borja appeared alongside John, calling out to everyone on deck in a language John did not understand. His presence seemed to calm the living who started to end their panicked behavior. The more he talked, the more the freed slaves came to order and they lined up, ready to leave the *Lilith.*

"Clear the deck!" John said.

Zombies began throwing dead and half-dead crewmembers overboard.

Goliath appeared last and with him was Andrew. He looked as though he were about to collapse from overwhelming fear. He locked eyes with John and made a blood-curdling scream.

"Bring him here to me," John said.

Goliath escorted him over. John seized him by his arm and took him to the door to the captain's quarters. "Stand here."

"John, how are you alive?"

John turned back to the zombies, raised the cat of nine tails, and screamed. The zombies stopped what they were doing and gathered into a tight group with Borja and Goliath in the front. John pointed to the captain's quarters and the hoard moved as one. They struck the door in waves, trying to break it down. Gunshots erupted from the other side. Bullets ripped through the door and struck them. It had little effect on their attack. When the door was finally breached, they rushed in, destroying the quarters before getting hold of Captain Hawkins and bringing him out onto the deck before John. They forced him to his knees.

"We've taken your cargo and your ship," John said.

"Go ahead and kill me," Captain Hawkins said. "You think I fear death?" He began to laugh. "You think I care what you'll do to me? I know what you are, and I say to your face I don't fear you!"

John produced the cat of nine tails and let the spiked ball swing before Captain Hawkins's eyes. He drew his arm back, prepared to strike, then stopped. He dropped the cat to the floor.

"You are to bring death to him," Borja said in a gravelly voice.

"He's been defeated by a mutt. I have brought a special kind of death to him." John turned to Andrew. "You and Corbin are the only witnesses to this. He is in the longboat. Take it and row away from this ship. When you are picked up, tell those who sail these seas that death rides upon these waters. Slavers should beware. Death and revenge will come for them. And its name is *Adroa*. Goodbye, my friend."

Andrew repeated "Adroa," nodded, and rushed to lower the longboat where he found Corbin still passed out. He climbed in and started to lower it. John waited until he heard the splash of the boat then he turned to Borja.

"I took his livelihood. You can take his life. Kill him."

As the zombies closed in, John walked away. He heard Borja groan and Captain Hawkins scream as the army tore him apart. One grabbed the cat of nine tails and beat what was left of him until there was nothing but a bloody pile of flesh.

John helped the remaining living slaves board the *Adroa.*

He and the others grabbed lanterns, set the *Lilith* a blaze, returned to their ship, and quietly sailed away into the night.

The End

A CONFUSION OF THE GODS

SUMIKO SAULSON

Zeus let out a stolid rumble of discontent that rattled the blue-gray clouds surrounding Mount Olympus. Níðhöggr the corpse-sucker let out a wicked cackle of laughter that shook the shores of Náströnd. In Guineé, a sly grin tilted one corner of Papa Legba's mouth. The rotting corpses of the dead had risen and were busy trotting across the Earth, and all of the Gods of Death, not to mention a few Gods of Life, wanted to know who was responsible.

"You've got to be freaking kidding me!" Anubis shouted, deeply perturbed by the reanimation of so many mummies. Many still lay hidden in their tombs, not yet unearthed by pesky and disrespectful Englishmen. But King Tut — having been returned to his grave in the Valley of the Kings — had risen in a froth of adolescent rage and hunger, and torn off the nose of a helpful, but unfortunate, tour guide with his teeth before scrambling after the tourists.

"Serves them right," Osiris said with a shrug. "I say the living really ought to have left the dead to rest. Then, they would not be having such problems."

Ereshkigal frowned. "Is this some doing of that new upstart God, Jehovah? I've heard about his shenanigans with Lazarus and his son...what's his name...oh yeah, that Jesus character?"

"I'm sure Jesus was a one-off," her sukkal Namtar responded, calmly tapping on his computer keyboard. Sukkal are advisors, and often diplomats. Ereshkigal was important enough to have one, being the First Lady of Irkalla, the Babylonian underworld, and all that.

"This probably isn't Jehovah, then..." Ereshkigal's daughter, Nungal, said. "This thing is happening with all kinds of Dead, all over the planet. I've been watching videos about it on Tik-Tok."

Ereshkigal narrowed her eyes. "Well, if he isn't responsible, then he's sure to blame *us* for it. That one! Always going on about Babylon this, Sumeria that."

Now, the Dead far outnumber the living, what with there being fifteen dead people for every single one that is still alive. Having resurrected all at once, their rising created a huge problem for the living. It would have been a larger problem still if all of the Dead had been in the position to hunt and kill the living. But, as it was, many of them had already rotted away into nothing.

And then some were cremated. Sure, Grandma's pissed-off urn angry-rattling itself off the mantle and crashing onto the floor was disturbing, but unless you got a concussion from an unlucky strike to the head, it was unlikely to kill you. Some human scientists feared that particles like these, of the long-dead or those incinerated unto ash, would somehow collect and attack the living. Most, however, were more concerned with the immediate problem at hand.

The freshly dead were the biggest problem. 8,295 people die every day in the United States. Needless to say, some places are more prone to generating the freshly dead. Take nursing homes, for example. The backs of ambulances. Emergency rooms, and intensive care units. And you only really needed one dead person for an outbreak to occur.

This created huge problems for medical workers, as well as for news anchors trying to cover the situation, especially in the beginning. Meg Ward, with the Channel 5 Evening News up in Ukiah, was covering a story about all of the injured overcrowding the hospital emergency rooms when a man coded while he was being loaded off of an ambulance. Shrieks filled the airwaves as his angry teeth tore off the arm of a paramedic trying to secure his oxygen mask. Moments later, his corpse lurched off of the gurney, grabbed the second paramedic, and bit open the back of his skull as he tried to run away. Meg Ward's cameraman leaned in and got a great shot of the zombie eating the man's brains. He was so busy filming it that he didn't notice the first paramedic, having bled to death, rise up out of the ambulance and sink his teeth deep into his carotid artery as his camera toppled to the floor, where it continued to film the ensuing bloodbath.

The next problem was those who were not yet buried. Tons of dead folks not yet cremated or buried sitting around funeral parlors or in morgues. Being embalmed didn't seem to stop them from resurrecting or anything. It just made it so they didn't rot as quickly. Teeth are very durable — one of the last parts of the body to decay. Contrary to popular belief, most morticians do not sew the mouths of the dead closed. They use two screws, held together by a single wire, which are easily pulled apart by the dead. However, in the rarer case where they do, the hungry dead are more than happy to tear their own lips to tatters removing the sutures in their ravening lust to feast upon their first meal of living flesh. Conveniently for the dead, some morticians use a cream or gel to keep the lips from parting in the coffin. Very easy to unseal.

You may be wondering who I am, and how I know so many

things. Well, I'm not a God or anything like that. My name is Sam, and I'm the fourth Horseman of the Apocalypse, Death. I've been at a meeting for the Gods and other emissaries of Death. I mean, we aren't all Gods, you know. And Jehovah doesn't have time to show up at all of these little meetings, and besides… he's a jealous God, not about to try to meet with all these beings he considers self-aggrandizing peons. So I came.

Technically, my name is Samael, but that's so formal. You can just call me Sam.

As for how I showed up, well, Jehovah sent me with Hades. Which sounds weird because he's a jealous guy, and you know, Hades is the Greek God of the Underworld. But the two religions kept getting combined and so somehow or other, we ended up in a two-man show during the apocalypse in Revelation 6:7–8. I don't know if this is that, but since we showed up together, you never really know.

Or, did Hades send me? I'm honestly not sure, because all of these religions keep getting mixed together and culturally appropriating one another. Who can keep track? I mean, Ereshkigal is both a Babylonian and Sumerian Goddess from Mesopotamia, but also a Greek Goddess, although the Greeks call her Hecate. She was also worshiped in Alexandria, Egypt. There, Ereshkigal, Hecate, and Hermecate were invoked separately in the Greek Magical Papyri. So why wouldn't I be in more than one religion? These humans keep traveling, intermingling, and converting each other or just sharing practices. That is…when they aren't busy going to war.

And you might think that the raising of the Dead would make it so they could all join forces against one common enemy, but no. Different religions are interpreting this differently, so yeah, naturally, yet more of the religious wars. So, I am here at this great summit of the Gods, listening to oh so much bickering.

And I'm here with a great big secret.

I know who is responsible for all of this. My guess? It's my big brother, Claude. He's also known as the First Horseman of the Apocalypse. You may know him by the name Pestilence, or possibly Plague. Honestly, they mean pretty much the same thing. Historically, he has been responsible for things like the Bubonic Plague, the AIDS Pandemic, Spanish Influenza, and Leprosy. His most recent works include Mpox, and the COVID-19 Epidemic. Well, believe it or not: Zombiism is pathogen based. And I know for a fact that he is also responsible for the Zombie Plague.

As petty as he is, he did this all because he was pissed off, just because they didn't invite him to this party.

—

YOU SEE, it all started last week when I got my invitation to this meeting. It's an annual convention of the Gods of Death. The organizers keep moving it around. Last year it was in Dublin, but this year, it's going to be in Pittsburgh.

George A. Romero set a lot of his movies about zombies there. To be fair, that kind of thing influences the organizers a lot. This year, Yama, Bao Zheng, and Xipe Totec are the heads of the organizing team. Xipe Totec is both a death God and the master of plagues in the Nahua religion. And to be honest, Claude has always been insanely jealous of him. I mean, Claude is just a Horseman, he's not a God or anything. And like, even though I am also the Angel of Death, Jehovah greatly frowns upon that whole angel worship thing. I believe you've probably already heard about his falling out over the matter with our older brother, Lucifer. Bad news. I don't like pissing Dad off. I try to stay on his good side.

Going back to Xipe Totec, though... see, he's a huge George Romero fan. And that's why we held DeathCon in Pittsburgh this year. Old Xipe could not stop going on and on about how Zombiism in the Romero universe was a form of plague--in most modern zombie iterations, for that matter. Now originally, they were religious in nature, a fact that Papa Legba never will let anyone forget. But the government-lab-disease zombies and the organic-nature-disease kind have sort of taken over the genre over the past fifty years, and this is largely due to George Romero.

Claude was naturally displeased when he heard about the Pittsburgh thing. He loved Romero almost as much as he hated Xipe. He started going off the minute I texted him about it. My brother was ranting some crazy crap about his impending ascension to Godhood, and how he'd get them all to recognize him at last. I quickly changed my mobile phone over to the Hades family plan, so we wouldn't get into shit with the big J. Claude arranged a meet-up with me at a local cemetery.

"Fucking posers!" Claude yowled as he waved his fingers over a grave. The headstone read "Margaret Jones, Beloved Wife, and Mother, December 3, 1904 - September 12, 1963". A thin wisp of swampy green gas erupted from the ground underneath his fingers. "I've been busting my ass with the whole COVID-19 situation since 2020, but no one gives me credit. They've all got their heads so far up Xipe's ass that they can't see anything except his lower intestine. I heard they credited him for the pandemic. Probably why he got to choose the con location this year."

"I've mostly heard them blaming the actual year, 2020," I said with a shrug. "D&D geeks were joking that it was the year the Universe finally confirmed the crit."

"They want a plague? I'll show 'em a plague!" Claude screamed, completely ignoring me, twitching his pale, bony fingers ever more furiously. I heard the rotted capstone crack below us, and a mummified hand shot up out of the grave. Margaret's withered flesh looked like a weather-beaten old brown leather handbag. All of her fat had rotted off, leaving only tendon and bone under the desiccated flesh. Another hardened talon of a hand quickly ripped through the rest of the grave. The hands planted themselves on separate sides of the tomb and struggled to pull the rest of Margaret out of the dirt.

"This might take a long time," I observed, doing my best to keep my voice calm. I love Claude, but he was into some dark mojo right now. I mean, necromancy. Nothing to play with. Not that the actual Death Gods didn't do that sort of thing all the time. And I suppose that's what Claude now aspires to be.

—

I WALKED in through the back gate of the Anti-Zombie Incursion volunteer station, which had been hastily erected by the California National Guard. As I recall it, this station had been a restaurant of some kind before the COVID-19 Pandemic: one that took up half of the damned block. It went out of business during shelter-in-place. For a while, they'd used it as an impromptu shelter for the homeless, a place where they could bathe up and avoid the infection. Now, what used to be a parking lot was surrounded by hastily-erected link fencing, rolls of barbed wire mounted at the top to discourage any particularly bright and ambitious zombies from attempting to crawl over. It looked like a prison.

The restaurant building was filled with lockers and stations where we could suit up, and pick up our arms and ammunition for a fun day of zombie slaying. As I walked into the front door, I caught a glimpse of myself in a mirror, mounted high overhead in some earlier time, when the workers had to be concerned with armed robbery, shoplifters, or dine-and-dash thieves. There I stood in my most recent incarnation: a tall, lanky, yet baby-faced African American man in his very early twenties.

Although we were immortal, Dad made sure that we didn't attract unwanted attention by having our human guises age at a normal rate and change once they reached whatever the current human lifespan was. We began each cycle as fully grown adults, so I'd had this model for a couple of years now and would continue for another sixty years or so with him. Father had granted me this visage back in 2020, at the start of the pandemic. He is all-seeing and all-knowing, so I have to imagine he was aware we'd be dealing with this whole zombie situation.

"Mask up!" the human woman screamed at her troops, pulling her N-95 mask up over her mouth and nose, and her clear plastic visor down over her eyes to demonstrate. Then she lifted the visor and pulled off the mask, shouting, "Haven't you morons learned anything from 2020?"

Her name was Rochelle. The man standing closest to her, Sean, released a roof-shaking peal of laughter. He patted the gasmask that sat perched on the top of his skull. "I think I got this, boss!"

A glance around the room revealed a variety of plastic goggles, painter's masks, and the like. Most of them were armored, encased ankle-to-wrist in thick denim or canvas. The mortals knew they had to keep zombie blood out of their mouths, eyes, and any cuts on their bodies to avoid the risk of infection. One guy was tightly wrapped in a rubber kink suit, with only the eyes and the mouth cut out. He wore goggles over his eyes and a plastic shield mask over his mouth. I knew him... what was his name again? Max.

"Whatchu lookin' at, Sam?" Max hollered from across the room, rubbing his crotch suggestively. "You wanna find out what the suit is for?"

"Oh no, I'm good," I said, checking the seal on my own painter's mask. I was here to gather information for the council — not to get into it with this knucklehead. And then...I had to do it all without accidentally snitching off my reckless and power-mad brother. I know what you're thinking: Claude and I have a codependent relationship. Well, you're not wrong. Claude is the first Horseman of the Apocalypse, and I am the fourth. How can I ever achieve my grand purpose if he mucks it all up? From that point of view, I guess it's less brotherly protectiveness and more a sense of self-preservation on my part.

"Shut the hell up!" Rochelle barked at Max, giving him a magnificent side-eye. "It's hard enough getting volunteer troops down here in the first place, without your nasty ass chasing them off."

Max grunted and gave her a nod but flipped her off the minute she turned her back. She caught it in the mirror above. She lifted her hand and gave him the one-finger salute. "You know I can see you, right? Dumb ass."

"Sorry..." he responded sheepishly.

"Sorry don't cut it," she said. "You're getting written up." She pulled out a pad and started scribbling something into a form.

"What are you looking at?" she said, staring at me now. "Grab a weapon and get your ass out to the truck, kid! Before they take off without you!"

I nodded and quickly did as I was told. Soon, I was in the back of a transport vehicle, headed out to Colma.

Most people who are not from the San Francisco Bay Area are completely unfamiliar with Colma, California. It's a city best known for two things: being the filming location for the 1971 movie *Harold and Maude,* and housing most of San Francisco's dead. San Francisco is a seven-square-mile overcrowded city that has forbidden any new human burials within its walls since 1900. San Francisco, in a shockingly sacrilegious move, deconsecrated the remaining graves and unceremoniously evicted the dead in 1912 because the city was overcrowded. A massive number of the dead were moved to Colma, the City of San Francisco's personal graveyard.

Not at all the place you'd want to be living in case of the zombie apocalypse. This is why all of the residents of Colma were evacuated, and a high fence, topped with razor wire, was built around the border of the cemetery-infested city. Nowadays, Colma was a township of zombies. Starving revenants who wandered the maze of abandoned malls and funeral parlors in an increasingly frustrating hunt for the flesh of the living.

The San Bruno Mountains created a high natural barrier on one side of Colma. On the other side, the unfortunate residents of Daly City kept a wide berth, having evacuated a mile-wide swath of territory known as the Colma Borderlands. The Borderlands was a militarized zone insulating the denizens of Daly City from their new zombie neighbors. It was fenced off on either side. Within it, a massive mall had been converted into the Serramonte Deployment Center.

It took about twenty minutes for the transport vehicle to arrive at the Serramonte Deployment Center in Daly City. From there, we climbed onto the floor in our jackboots and lined up, rifles on our shoulders, to prepare for the march to Colma.

"We got a climber!" Rochelle shouted into her walkie-talkie. I looked up to see a recently deceased older gent in a filthy gray suit, a series of gashes displaying flayed flesh between rips rent by razorwire. "Copy that!" Max shot back.

As his glazed yellow eyes took us in, the dead man inhaled

deeply, as if catching a whiff of a freshly cooked steak. His rotting lips moistened as he began to visibly drool. Completely mesmerized by this display of gluttony, I stood there and stared as the zombie began to pick up speed.

Max raised his rifle, caught it in his sights, and quickly dispensed of the thing with a highspeed round to the head. Zombie brains splattered on the bright yellow brick of the mall corridor before us and began to ooze slowly down the wall, leaving streaks of rust-red blood.

"I hope you do more shooting and less staring out in the field," Max said, fixing me with a pointed glance.

I swallowed hard and then nodded. "Yes, sir."

"Enough chitter chatter!" Rochelle bellowed, "get your asses in line. Get ready to roll out!" She pointed to two white lines, painted on the floor, and ordered us to line up behind each of them. All around me, groups of humans of all genders, races, and sizes, and a surprisingly broad variation in age began to arrange themselves in two lines. It seems that everyone who was physically up to zombie slaying wanted to sign up. All of them wore some kind of eye and mouth covering, gloves, and boots. Some of them wore various kinds of rubber or leather gear under or over their camouflage uniforms. But all of them wore uniforms.

As we lined up to walk, a couple of familiar faces emerged beside me. On one side, was Papa Legba, looking remarkably down-to-Earth in his army fatigues and jackboots. On the other side of me was Osiris, looking regal and aloof despite the very same military wear.

"You are fooling no one, son!" Papa Legba hissed under his voice, locking step with me as Rochelle ordered us on our one-mile march towards the Colma border. "You and your white God have something to do with this."

"I promise you that Jehovah hasn't caused any of this," I assured him, relieved that he had said nothing about Claude.

"Xipe Totec said that your brother Claude was acting weird," Osiris said, pulling up behind me. Claude, by the way, comes from a Latin word meaning "one with a limp or stutter", which is why claudication is a symptom associated with peripheral artery disease. Roman emperor Claudius was given the name due to his affliction, and soon thereafter my brother, Mashḥit, acquired the name for himself. Over time, though, it was shortened to Claude. Osiris, however, pronounces it like "clod."

"That's correct," a snooty-looking man with a hound-like face said, suddenly appearing beside Osiris and directly behind Papa Legba, as we were marching in rows of two. This was Anubis. Why was he here now? Was this some kind of a Death God intervention? Another, impromptu this time, convention?

Just then, everything grew eerily silent as we approached the Colma border. The dazed men said not a word, as the throng of ravenous zombies came into view, amassing upon the opposite side of the fence, which they pushed against, threatening to push it over. Rochelle ordered us to prepare our weapons, and so we did… eyes on the prize as she shouted our orders. "One. Two. Three. Fire!"

My prizewinning shot zipped through the air and landed smack dab in the jaundiced eye of an ambling deadman, causing it to explode in a firework of red gore before searing through his brain and ripping off the back of his skull.

"Nice shot," Osiris said approvingly, watching as his own landed seconds later on a zombie coming up to the rear of mine, lodging squarely into her forehead before tearing off most of her scalp.

"Clear!" Rochelle shouted. "Those of you at the front, into the trenches!"

Twenty feet away from the fence, there were trenches. To the front of them, facing the fence, were heavy bags of soil behind which a soldier could hide, rifle sights trained upon the zombies on the other side of the gate. Rochelle waved the first two dozen of us into those trenches. Naturally, I ended up in a trench with these pesky Death Gods: Papa Legba, Anubis and Osiris.

"Isn't Azrael the real Angel of Death?" Anubis hissed.

"There's more than one of us," I said, blushing at the sudden unwanted attention.

"The Abrahamic religions are so confusing," Osiris remarked. "As I recall, Samael is the Angel of Death in Judaism, while Azrael the Angel of Death in Islam. There's some crossover between Judaism, Islam, and Christianity. That's why they define things a bit differently.

"Don't the Jews and the Christians call you Lucifer?" Papa Legba purred, smiling seductively.

"Perhaps, at times. But it's not accurate. We aren't the same person at all," I sighed. "They just hate death. Besides, humans are always conflating things, you see. Not to mention misinterpreting and improperly translating them. Satan is a title, meaning adversary. I was given the title because as the Angel of Death, I was an adversary of the people. Lucifer Morningstar was also given the title satan. So, we were both called satan, but we aren't the same person. Unlike Lucifer, I have remained faithful to the Lord. Lucifer is the adversary of Jehovah God."

"Have you actually been faithful, though?" Anubis insinuated. "I don't know what your brother is up to, but aren't you involved with it? And didn't you just say that Jehovah never condoned it?"

Why was Anubis being so hostile all of a sudden? Every time I took a breath, he was shading me for some reason. Completely unwarranted.

"I am not a fallen angel!" I protested. "I am the Fourth Horseman of the Apocalypse. You can't fall while you follow God's plan. I am following Jehovah's plan."

"You're creeping me out," Osiris said. "Please miss me with all of that Revelation crap. Can we just get back to zombie slaying?"

He lifted his rifle and blasted the skull off of a mummified corpse in a sunny peach pantsuit. I couldn't help but wonder, who buried their dead in *that*?

"Hah ha!" Papa Legba hooted, watching the kill. "Polyester. Those who died in the 70s can expect their pantsuits to survive several hundreds of years after their flesh and bones have fallen to dust."

"I thought the Fourth Horseman's name was Thanatos," Anubis said saltily.

"That literally just means Death in Greek," I said, feeling very frustrated. "I mean, what's your point, dude?"

"I think he's just fucking with you," Osiris said, popping the head off of another walker.

"Or trying to catch you in a lie," Papa Legba said bluntly, popping off a round into the knees of a row of inbound dead. He didn't go for the kill shot. He got sadistic pleasure out of maiming them and fell into a bout of wicked laughter as they all toppled to the ground in front of the fence. The wounded dead began crawling on their hands and knees, desperate to taste human flesh.

"What would I have to lie about?" I said unconvincingly.

"Revelation clearly states that you, the Fourth Horseman, will unleash war, famine, pestilence, and wild beasts upon mankind during your white God's so-called end days," Papa Legba said with a smirk.

"Literally just the end of the Roman Empire, though," I said, doing my best to act bored. "And that already fell."

"Like the Roman Catholic Church doesn't exist?" Osiris said, capping a slowly encroaching corpse in full military regalia with one neat shot.

"See? This shady, sneaky crap is why I suspect you," Anubis said, slinging around so that his rifle was suddenly facing me.

"Oh come on!" I bellowed like an injured bull. "If you kill me,

I'll just have to get a new body. I've only had this one for three years. Don't be petty!" I looked around, desperate for Rochelle or Max to stop this nonsense, but we were in the trenches and they couldn't see us.

"We know you command your brother," Papa Legba said, raising an eyebrow. "Your own God snitched on you. Why don't you stop lying?"

"Ugh," Osiris said. "I'm tired of hearing this garbage. Why don't you just shoot him already?"

"That's cold!" I said.

I was about to say something else when the air began to reverberate before me. The earth trembled, and I could hear the sound of a distant bell chiming. This kind of thing only happened when an archangel appeared. I was absolutely terrified. Was Anubis right? Had I messed up somehow, pissed off Jehovah?

I was standing behind him as he began to manifest, his long white feathers mere inches from my face. I was confused. Why was he facing Anubis rather than me? Had he come to protect me?

"Fuck you, Anubis!" the angel shouted with a distinct lack of decorum. "Fuck you, and fuck Xipe Totec, too!"

"Claude?" I asked, stunned.

"Samael doesn't give me orders!" he yelled at Anubis. Then he turned around and yelled at me so hard I could feel his spittle hit my face. "I don't take orders from you, Sam! You just shut up!"

"So, this was all your doing, then?" Osiris said, not lifting his head up from his gun sight as he lined up another zombie kill. "Not your brother Sam? Not your God Jehovah?"

"It was all me!" Claude bragged, turning to face Anubis. "You all give Sam credit for everything. You all think you're so important! Well, I'm just as good as you. And I did this plague! Why don't you go ahead and tell that to Xipe Totec!?"

Just then, I felt a hot gush of blood splash my face and heard a round reverberate like thunder as Anubis shot Claude right in the face. His head exploded just like one of those zombies. And I heard the bullet whistle past my ear.

"Your brother always was an asshole," Papa Legba chuckled.

"Nice shot," I said, finally emerging from my state of shock, and lifted my arm to shake the hand of Anubis.

"Nah, I'm good," he said, winking at me. "It sure was easy getting your dumbass brother to confess. Missing you with the shot, though... that was just an accident."

"Your brother just caught a one-way ticket back to Jehovah," Osiris said, finally putting down his gun. "I'd like to see him explaining his bullshit to Big J. I remember how he reacted the last time one of y'all tried to become a God."

"Toodles!" Papa Legba said, snapping his fingers and disappearing.

"Yeah, we out," Anubis concurred, snapping his finger and vanishing as well.

I shrugged and turned to Osiris. "I guess you're going too now?"

"Oh hell naw," he said, raising his face up to the rifle sight again. "I ain't going nowhere! Not when I got me some zombies to kill."

The End

SIRABIRI OF THE RESTLESS

MOUSTAPHA MBACKÉ DIOP

Sirabiri observed from underground as the chief's wife ceremoniously prepared for her own death. She was pretty, that one. Deep-set brown eyes skimmed over her many servants; her tawny skin looked dull under the crimson lights that inundated the courtyard. The woman stood still as a statue, except for the episodic spasm that seized her chest: a hint of violently repressed sobs.

Like insects, the servants flew in and out of the large mud hut, which had a roof covered in shiny straw and walls lined with abstract, swirling patterns. They carried elegant white fabrics, bracelets of gold and silver, jars of rich-smelling *curaay*, and other precious things. Her oldest servant, wrinkles cut deep into her skin like bark lines, sat wailing in a corner. They all ignored her—and the unnatural creature that waited at the short straw fence.

All this, Sirabiri saw through that creature's eyes. A jackal, it was. Till was its name. Silky, sand-hued fur coated its emaciated build, and obsidian eyes sat deep into its skull.

The contents of the jackal's abdomen spilled from a large

gash in his golden fur: rotten, cold intestines that dangled like a vile necklace. Sensing the servants' muffled fear, which strangely did not hinder their movements, Sirabiri smiled. She was proud at how she made the jackal: covered in an almost-blinding beauty, putrefying on the inside. Dead and alive. One leg into the land of the living—where it heeded the wishes of those desperate enough to summon her. The other at her sides: an everlasting companion in sacred silence, among fat worms, sweet bones, and all the dreams that had dried inside them.

Outside, strings of faint, red light began dancing across the beige walls and under the bushes. As if on cue, the servants trickled away from the hut and vanished into the falling night. They couldn't have seen the red lights for what they truly were. But humans, Sirabiri had come to know, were often prompt to follow their instinct when it told them to flee.

The spirits had come. This was their hour, after all. This moment between dog and wolf, when it felt like holding one's breath before diving into dark waters. They thrived on ambiguity, and blind despair as the chief's wife exhibited. They'd seen Till but couldn't sense Sirabiri unless she wanted them to. With their concealed faces and raffia robes, the spirits were fickle beings. Their laughter irritated her, but she paid them no mind.

They could mock as they wanted. Sirabiri was the one who was born human and chose to become a goddess.

And that goddess had a task to complete.

"Dem na."

The chief's wife—who was now a widow and perhaps without child—began repeating those two words, over and over, "dem na," as she leaned forward and grabbed the old woman—her own wet nurse, it seemed—in her arms, both their faces streaked with tears. "Dem na," she muttered, forcing the *ndaa* between her gnarled hands. "Dem na," she stated in answer to her pleading eyes.

He's gone.

Dragging her feet across the dust-covered, rocky floor, the old woman floundered as if life had already left her body. After she'd splattered oil all around the inner and outer walls of the hut, she lit a candle and positioned herself at the door.

"Don't do this, Anta Sabel," she croaked.

The other woman went on muttering those words, which were more than a prayer. They were a battle cry, the only reason why she was ready to lay down her life.

Inside the hut and on top of a huge wooden trunk stood a statuette. The candle's flickering light illuminated the white-painted eyes and the deep mahogany tint it was covered in. Goat's blood, surely, from the one they'd sacrificed at dawn in honor of the summon. The statuette had a protruding belly and held a tiny glass shard that welcomed Anta Sabel's blood as she pressed a finger upon it.

It was almost a kiss, so heavy with devotion that Sirabiri had no choice but to listen.

"They have taken my only child—the white men with their boots and death machines, the ones that killed my husband. Now, they will kill Mulay too, even though he's just a boy. They will cook and eat him, the devils. Or turn him into one. I do not know..." A sob burst from her quivering lips, wet with tears. Something was breaking inside her. Perhaps it already had.

Floating inside of the hut, the thick *curaay* smoke coated the back of her throat. "I give myself to you, O Goddess. You who forsook your flesh and beating heart to embrace the quiet of the tomb. You, who listen to the cries of those who have been wronged. You who rise from the hereafter as their executor." The statuette, as well as the precious offerings brought earlier, seemed to disappear as shadows crept along the walls and engulfed them. All noises were as if sucked in, and a blanket of darkness covered the woman. "Accept this vessel and strike your judgment upon my son's captors."

Outside, the old woman's shaking hand let go of the candle she was holding. Then she stumbled away, forcing herself not to look back. She had cried and begged all she could, for this daughter of hers, this *mother*, who was about to make the ultimate sacrifice for the one she loved most. For the only one she had left.

The white flames were ravenous. Of the offerings and Anta Sabel's kneeling body, they didn't lick a hair. But they consumed everything else: buffalo skins that her husband, Chief Mory, had hung on their walls—spoils of his own hunting parties, he liked to remind her with a crooked smile—the *tengaade,* with cowries and threads of copper laced around its tip, which he'd wanted to pass on to their son. The fire left nothing of the bed they'd shared, imprinted with memories of hushed laughter in the middle of the night, of arguments that faded within hours under his gentle touch. Behind her tightly-shut eyes, Anta Sabel saw Mory's face, his coarse beard through which blood pooled, and his eyes that yelled, "Keep him safe!" before they turned cold.

She hadn't been strong enough to protect Mulay. But something else would do it in her stead. The ritual had to work before it was too late. One last tear rolled down Anta Sabel's cheek. She gripped the statuette's legs. She sucked in a breath, then jammed the statuette right through her belly, screaming as the glass cut through her white garments, her skin, and found her beating heart.

"Avenge us, Sirabiri of the Restless. Avenge *me.*"

* * *

This would not be the first time Sirabiri walked the earth. Noblewomen, like Anta Sabel, had ordered for a screaming slave to be restrained in their chambers, so Sirabiri could use their body to avenge the death of their husbands, or to eliminate troublesome obstacles to their succession. Warriors had captured enemies and summoned her into their bodies, so she could be allowed access to their generals and end wars from within. She couldn't possess a dead body, no. A life had to be taken for her to rise. When, through her tears, Anta Sabel had dug up the infamous statuette, many a servant had offered to be her sacrifice, seeing how grief-stricken their kind mistress was.

It had surprised Sirabiri when the woman chose to end her own life, instead. It was selflessness, and such a natural thing for a love so true. The kind to which death could not turn a blind eye.

She would strike.

* * *

THERE WAS a black worm wriggling through the soft, blood-soaked floor. It was large, almost the size of a grass snake, and it made its way through the surface slowly. The worm entered Anta Sabel's mouth as her soul fled it, hauled to a new destination. Bursting into a thousand particles, it settled into the woman's muscles, stretching and respiring and making itself comfortable until Anta Sabel's corpse was its.

Then, her eyes—milky-white, burning with a thirst for retaliation—flew open. Till trotted inside the remnants of what had been Chief Mory and Anta Sabel's hut. Ashes stained its paws as it bowed before the corpse and waited. The jackal observed, as it rose to its feet with unnatural creakings and bent limbs.

"Welcome back, mistress," Till said, in that low, shrill tone that would have driven any human mad. The corpse grunted and hobbled away from the ash, picking up a huge, soot-covered stone that it smashed against its right leg. Frightened by the thundering noise, clouds of birds cleared out nearby trees in a frenzy.

"I thank you, Till," Sirabiri replied, in a gravelly voice lower than the one Anta Sabel had spoken in. The goddess ran a pale-skinned hand through its silky fur; she grazed the soft intestines with a finger and a twisted smile slit open the jackal's mouth. Making a few steps forward, she relished in the new shape of her leg: bent inward, in the curve Sirabiri had been born with when she was human.

Before she had met Taxawaalu and chosen the gift of godhood.

* * *

"WHERE TO?"

Till's voice redirected her focus toward the task at hand. A half-moon lit up the clear sky above their heads, and there was silence in the warm air. Creatures of the night, who would usually be searching around for food or a mate at this hour, seemed to be observing Sirabiri. With her angular, dry gait and the shadows that clung to her immaculate garments, she might have been a mystery to them. Someone who was not from their world, but walked as if she held all its secrets in her closed mouth.

Hints of a sob brushed her ear. It came not from a living soul, but from the shadows always hovering around her. Sirabiri knew them for what they were: a small fragment of the pleader's soul, left behind to guide her to whoever she needed to punish. Anger burned in her chest as she scoured through Anta Sabel's last memories, filled with gunshots and the cries of a boy separated from his mother. For now, she chose to leave them aside.

Sirabiri was walking amongst the living, and she had a blood debt to collect.

"There is still the matter of the kidnappers' location. Perhaps someone in the village would know the way they went."

The goddess and the jackal dove deeper into the night. Fallen branches cracked under their step as they passed by a cluster of tamarind shrubs that rustled under soft winds, beneath which whispered the spirits inhabiting it. Now that she was above once more, they seemed to always be watching her, commenting on her every decision. The spirits were mere incarnations of Nature: a current of twirling wind here, rocks at the edge of a crossroad there. Sirabiri was more than that, even being born as a human, and they must have feared her as much as they resented her for what she'd become.

She steered clear of the village Chief Mory and Anta Sabel used to lead. Unless it was absolutely necessary, she wouldn't want to impose the sight of their recently-deceased ruler upon them. Till was right—for all she knew, they could already be at sea or trampling another village. It would be faster to seek help from the villagers, especially since her time on this plane was limited. But Sirabiri knew of another way.

"I have never been with child," she said in a whisper. "But I am wearing the body of a mother. And mothers always know where to find their children."

So, she tugged at a point deep inside her abdomen. Playing with it, rolling it between imaginary fingers. Nothing happened, at first. She had just arisen and was still adjusting to Anta Sabel's body, with all its pain and dizzying thirst for retribution. The beaming face of a young Chief Mory slowly came to mind, like the sketch of an oil painting. His slender arms were cradling a wailing baby, which would only be silenced by warm breast milk filling his mouth. The baby, who later became a lanky, soft-eyed boy, had brought infinite joy into their house—until the Europeans shattered it.

Mulay...

Sirabiri and Till's bodies disintegrated into a thick cloud of iron-colored smoke as the goddess spoke the stolen child's name.

She knew the path that would lead them to him, but Sirabiri needed to use one of her most consuming abilities to arrive quickly.

You see, death was everywhere. Bones were scattered before a farm dog's kennel, which welcomed the smoke and hurled it toward the next jumping site, startling the scrawny dog that bayed at the moon. A porcupine's half-eaten, maggot-crawling carcass gave Sirabiri the boost she desired. It made her stronger, faster, when they moved on to a kettle of vultures that shrieked and rejoiced as they felt her under their skin. Vultures were a crucial part of death's inescapable cycle—they consumed what it left behind so that life could grow. In the night air, the smoke infiltrated and bounced from one to another, sliding through with a vertiginous speed, until they found the Europeans' camping site.

Their fire camps illuminated the night as voices resounded from tents left ajar. Less than ten of them, scattered over the bank of a stream that flowed slowly, carrying toad and cicada songs. Observing, Sirabiri and her jackal fused into the shadows. A man lifted the flap of one, leaving it with a thunderous laugh. He was tall, with muddy-brown hair, white skin, and crooked teeth. The stench of cheap liquor and grime emanated from him as he tramped toward the water, dropped his trousers, and released himself, right where they stood.

That angered her. Inebriation might have given leeway to his idiocy, but it was proof. For these men, any moment was suitable to soil and insult a land they already saw as rightfully theirs. They would hurt and kill their way through it. They'd piss on it and tap each other's shoulders, grinning while its people wailed.

"How dare you?"

He jerked his head upward, letting the last drops of urine stain his boots. Confronted with so much arrogance exhibited by such *mediocre* men, it was impossible for Sirabiri to contain herself. "How dare you?" she growled, again.

Anxiously, the man scanned the shadow and still couldn't see where the voice came from. All it took was a spastic nod from her, and Till prowled forward. She rejoiced in the terror that submerged his entire face at their sight: the jackal whose obscene beauty was phenomenal in death, and the woman in white, with an open wound across her abdomen and a smile that promised agony.

In seconds, Till pounced on his chest and sent him sprawling on the ground. Shrieks tore through the quiet night as the jackal ripped through the man's skin with razor-sharp teeth, digging until it found his gallbladder. It pierced it.

Sirabiri couldn't silence the man's screams, either; she had little power over the mind of the living. They died down quickly, not before the other men scurried from the tents, rifles in hand to take down whatever was attacking their camp. Torches, stretched forward, illuminated Till as it wolfed down the tiny, bitter organ. Upon the sight of their dead comrade, they began emptying their guns on the stoic jackal. Bullets prickled its skin like needles. The air grew heavy with smoke and sharp orders barked in their strange language.

All was cut short when, slowly, the dead man sat up.

* * *

SIRABIRI BELIEVED that everything was a blessing and a curse. Knowing their weapons and schemes offered them superior power, the white men came from the other side of the ocean to control this wild, rich land that was ripe for the taking. They reveled in the freedom of ransacking, stealing, and killing as they pleased. In their eyes, it was a twisted, unholy blessing to be gods in the eyes of black-skinned men.

She was going to be their curse. A reminder that death was unboth-

ered by the living's plots or power. That death might come late, but it would come for everyone.

* * *

CHAOS WAS BREAKING LOOSE. The men's fingers were tight against the triggers, and with no aim, they fired abundantly, shaking with fear. The jackal was taking them down, one by one. It grew taller, standing on its hind legs with black saliva oozing from its lips. The bullets drilled into his flesh caused no pain, nor did they slow it down. Eyes burning in the night, Till collected their unspeakable organs with devotion, allowing Sirabiri, from where she stood, to reach through her servant and into their dead flesh, pulling the strings that raised them to their feet. It came as easy as clapping her fingers. The dead became an extension of herself, a new set of unmoving eyes, of desiccated and obedient limbs. No order, voiced from within her soul into their corpses, would go unanswered. This gift had been bestowed upon her centuries ago as she had taken her last breath. Every time she'd use it, the solemn face of a wooden mask would come to her mind. Hints of what looked like pride, in no way visible in its look, folds of midnight-tinted raffia rags that always eluded her...

For the first time, Sirabiri noticed that there were Africans among them: wearing similar linen trousers and wrinkled chemises, they had dropped to the ground, their arms thrown above their heads. They might not know what she was, but they knew better than to confront her: most Africans understood that there was mystery and danger in the Unseen. Why had they chosen to side with the colonizers? Out of greed? Fear? She didn't know. Anger settled behind her sternum, mixed with anguish that wasn't her own. Even for a being that always dwelled in darkness, the smoke and the roars made by the guns made it harder for her to focus. Grating her even more were the spirits: they kept fluttering around her head, hidden under red beams of light that wouldn't go away.

She could feel Anta Sabel's son somewhere inside the camp.

The boy wasn't dead.

Find him.

Half of the twenty-something men that had fought against them had become her servants. The goddess saw through their unblinking, dull eyes as they crawled away from the battle, while Till finished the rest of the living ones off, sparing the African men only when they didn't rise as a threat. The Restless would twitch their limbs with every step. They crept into each tent, sniffing and groaning like boars. Infusing motion back into her rigid limbs, she followed in their wake.

She'd spent too much energy taking control of them. It was as if her vision had been fractured into ten: seeing stacked iron trucks from one lens, dying wax candles and discarded guns from the other. Already she felt darkness tugging at her skin. The earth was calling her back to rest in its embrace, clogging her joints with molasses. How hard would it be to give up? She was exhausted, overstimulated by the living world when death had been so quiet, so *simple*. Yet she couldn't disregard Anta Sabel's suffering, her sacrifice, especially when a shadow of the bereaved woman's soul still cried inside her ears. Sirabiri refused to surrender until her search had come to an end.

And it did.

"Ah." She sighed, her hand thrown over the balding head of a bulky man on all fours. The corpse, with viscera dangling from a deep slash in its belly, was positioned before a tent at the far end of the camp, which was cleverly assembled around the trunk of a young cashew tree.

Back to its normal stature, the jackal returned at her sides, its muzzle dripping with blood. "Have they found him, Mistress?"

"Yes. But it seems we have a problem."

Together they swiped the tent's opening to the side and went in. Poorly lit by a pair of kerosene lamps, it was searing-hot and empty of the clutter that filled the other tents.

Mulay had been forced on his knees, the back of his hands tied to the tree's trunk with metallic chains. He was slightly older than she expected—perhaps the horror of the last few days had forced it on him. His eyes bulged with fear. Sweat and dried tears coated his peanut-brown skin.

With a gaze colder than any she'd ever seen, a European man had a pocket gun pointed above Mulay's clavicle.

* * *

THE GODDESS CURSED under her breath. Growling, Till tensed up like a bow, ready to strike.

"Say the word, Mistress. And the white man will be yours."

"No. Stand back."

Now, Sirabiri struggled to stay awake. She had spoken to Till through their connected minds, but the white man eyed them, squinting. He squeezed his other hand on Mulay's shoulder, and his hold on the weapon didn't falter, even though he might have guessed that all his men were either dead or had deserted. He was alone, yet feigned composure as he faced the half-putrefying corpse of a jackal, a woman with milky-white eyes that were nothing but natural, and one of his men, brought back to life. With his slender frame and icy eyes, he might have been mistaken for someone as harmless as the boy he'd taken hostage.

Golden insignias caught the light on a vest, hanging by a paper-riddled desk on their right. Subtly, the man carried himself with arrogance. He didn't lead his men outside—instead, he chose to hide and keep an eye on what he'd thought the attackers were after. Time and time again, Sirabiri had been sent after men like him.

He was their general.

Till bared his teeth as the man shouted something in his language, staring down at them with anger… and a hint of fear that tasted like pepper on the tip of Sirabiri's tongue. That awakened her.

"Let the child go," she replied in Wolof. Mulay's breath quickened as his eyes grew even wider.

"Mother? Is that you?"

The goddess took one step forward, closer to the light, and the boy gasped, eyeing her curved leg underneath the white robes, her face where soft features had grown cruel. His shoulders collapsed, shaking with sobs. She ignored him.

"Whatever you are, stop right there. Or the boy dies!" the white man said in her language, butchering the words. Outside, bodies dropped with muffled thuds as Sirabiri was forced to cut the ties she'd controlled them with, keeping the last of her power close to her chest.

"Don't shoot." This was no negotiation. She was almost drained, and Till couldn't get to the man faster than those bullets. But she at least had to pretend she had everything under control, that she would pry Mulay from the white man's clutches before it was too late.

Miles seemed to separate her from Anta Sabel's son. The man licked beads of sweat atop his upper lip and began to twitch. Sensation in the lower part of her toes was dying, gravity hauling her closer. Sirabiri could no longer wait.

She yelled the mental command and turned into a cloud of smoke, going for the child as the jackal reached for the man's ankles with its claws…

Not fast enough.

The roar of the gun exploded along with the shriek of Anta Sabel's ghost.

* * *

In all the times she had risen from the ground, Sirabiri had longed for him. She wouldn't remember much after her missions in the land of the living—the darkness would cocoon her, welcoming her in a blanket of silence, and her worries would fade through the wet earth like the worms carve out a path from one end of life to the other. But even as soil and rock pressed against her skin, she could never forget him. She prayed for him to come when she walked above, she dreamed of him from below. It was a weird thing for a goddess to pray, and dream. Those were things humans did, because they lacked the power to shape their own destiny. To turn their desires into reality.

Sirabiri had the power. Yet, after all those years, her power failed to lead the only being she'd ever loved to her.

As his name said best, Taxawaalu had wandered away from her. He wasn't coming back.

* * *

When she shifted back to the body she'd borrowed, Sirabiri found herself clutching Mulay's shoulders, her hands stained with blood. The jackal rested his head on the boy's knees as if asleep. Looking around, she met the blank, blue eyes of the general, and the last of her anger faded at the sight of his mangled throat.

Still, it didn't matter. Blood oozing from above his clavicle, Mulay lifted his chin upward and looked at her.

"You are not my mother," he whispered.

"I am not."

Grief seized his entire body, even as he was dying. It was so pungent that it invaded her nostrils, turned her head to the boy and held it tight, telling her, "Don't look away." With her iron-solid fingers, Sirabiri crushed to flakes the chains restraining him. She wanted to reach through him and didn't know how. Never in all her callings did she stay around long enough to console the dead.

This time, she'd seen through everyone. She'd seen the gentle love that Chief Mory had covered his wife and boy with, which he'd left in the palm of their hands as one of the general's faceless men put a bullet in his body. And Anta Sabel had been fierce—it was embedded into these bones that Sirabiri wore. Even if she'd felt helpless in the face of guns, she'd laid down her life so the goddess could enact her vengeance.

So, Sirabiri tore a piece of her gown and pressed it against the bleeding shoulder in an iron grip. Slowing the hemorrhage as best as she could, she prayed for the one who would not come. There was no other way.

"Is she… gone? My mother? Is she at peace?"

"She is." Sirabiri never answered the last question. She couldn't bear to carve another wound into the boy's bleeding heart. In her arms, Mulay was growing as cold as she was. His chapped lips parted, faintly, as he took shallow breaths. She jerked him awake. "You can't fall asleep. Talk to me."

"What… are you?" Mulay whispered. There was a spark of resolve in his eyes, a certain resolve that he didn't inherit from his father, or his mother. It was his alone. The will to live.

"I am goddess," she stated. Her prayers went on, and still, Taxawaalu never came. "But I was human, first. I was the daughter of a mortician."

Till blew air from its nostrils and into the boy's legs, as if it too wanted him to stay afloat. The blood kept trickling through Sirabiri's fingers, albeit slowly. She raised her voice an octave, forcing Mulay to look her in the eyes as she spoke. "I would always stand by as families washed their departed ones and wept over them, no matter how my father yelled at me for sneaking into the cold, wet room. He'd given up, with time, and I was always there as he dug into the earth and laid a percale-shrouded body to rest. I was a child, younger than you are today."

"I won't grow much longer, though."

He coughed, and her fingers grew tight as her voice. "You will," she growled. Till licked Mulay's fingers with its cold tongue, and she shook him once again. "Stay with me!"

"How did you become a goddess?"

"Death fascinated me. When my father died, I continued his work, since I was his only child. And there was a shadow I'd see sometimes, right at the corner of my vision. People frowned upon a woman taking care of and burying their dead, saying that I would see things I wasn't supposed to see."

The boy was slipping away. For once, she loathed her familiarity with the other side. She felt it calling to him: the place she knew so well—or another version of it, perhaps. His parents could be waiting for him. There would be no pain, and it would all feel right.

It wasn't what Anta Sabel would have wanted.

For a moment, it seemed that the blood-soaked piece of cloth had stopped leaking. She kept putting pressure on it while being careful not to move her fingers too much. For a moment, she allowed herself to hope that the boy would live.

But, victim of her own exhaustion and her slipping hold on Anta Sabel's body, the muscles in her fingers loosened, and blood poured in rivulets down the boy's chest.

"I met him, the shadow. It was a spirit, you see. Not the kind that dances at twilight and does little more than scare you humans off, no. For eons, he'd wandered between worlds, between realities. Like I always did, he saw death as a transition: the grandest portal of them all. It intrigued him that I felt so at home with it. So I would talk, and he'd listen, just like I am talking to you now. In those days before the Europeans landed on our coasts, cruel nobles fought and plotted against each other, for power. Innocent people would be caught in the crossfire, but their murderers didn't care: not being burdened by morality was a freeway to more power. As I lowered corpses into the ground, among which many victims of unanswered crimes, I would tell him of my rage. I cared for the dead, for the way they and the justice they deserved were forgotten."

Sirabiri smiled, even though she did not think it possible. "It amused him, somehow. He wondered how one woman could topple unspoken decrees that predated humanity. He made a goddess out of me. Like the Spider, he skulked into people's dreams and taught them how to invoke me. He held my hand as I destroyed criminals, armies. Countries."

Still, Mulay watched her. Blood loss had drained the color off his lips. If you looked from afar, it would seem as if they were mother and child, whispering stories to each other as he rested his head on her bosom.

"I was in love with him," she confessed. "Even as I fell for him, he grew bored of me. So he left, in body and spirit. He could heal you now, if only he would come."

A cold wind seeped through the tent's opening. It threatened to knock the lamp off as it swirled around them. Her prayers and whatever faith she had in the wandering spirit were almost gone, as was the boy.

"They call him Taxawaalu," she whispered into the wind. And fury overcame her.

Aside from a nonchalant curiosity that pierced the veil of his boredom, she had never been anything to the spirit. This was a game to him. Surely, from the shadows of whatever universe he was strolling through, Taxawaalu was watching her, reveling in her helplessness. Despite all the power he'd gifted her, she couldn't be victorious this time. Perhaps it was in anticipation of this failure, this *human* ineluctability, that the masquerade had abandoned her.

Letting Mulay slide from her chest, Sirabiri opened her mouth and let out a long scream. Of an anger laced with longing, for as much as she hated Taxawaalu, there was always a hint of that noxious love anchored in her very being.

Mulay muttered something under his breath, but it never reached her ears. He shivered as more wind currents slid through the opening, intertwined with beads of red light. Knowing them for what they were—not the being she had begged so fervently to come—something fractured and set itself free within her body, within *her*.

The pesky spirit that had taunted her all evening would be its target.

With a snap, Sirabiri extended both arms forward, grasping the spirit midair and stripping it of its disguise. It had the appearance of a big-headed, stout man whose lips were curled in a rictus, its body covered in ragged, black fur. Its dark, wicked eyes sat deep in a hideous face, more animal than human.

The spirit was about to hurl insults at her face when she silenced it with another scream. This time, the ground screamed with her, along with the shadow of death that followed her every step. Something happened, then. Bursting in a cloud of crimson ashes, the spirit was... sucked into her gaping mouth.

Sirabiri tasted tar and rotting wood at the back of her throat. The spirit's power merged with her own, replenishing it. Till, her faithful companion, melted in a heap of dry bones and shining fur as the magic that had bonded it to her morphed into something *new*.

She did not understand it. Perhaps she wasn't meant to. The force of her anger, of her vulnerability, was such that looking down on Anta Sabel's arms, she couldn't help but wonder if she was in control, or if Anta Sabel was controlling her.

Mother?

That was what the boy had whispered, earlier. In the delirium that preceded him in death, he once again thought it was Anta Sabel who'd come to save him. Her face, which wasn't quite hers, would be the last he'd ever see.

The power felt foreign at the tip of her fingers. It wasn't made for her, not anymore. So the goddess did the only thing that seemed to make sense, that felt natural: she lowered her arms into Mulay's unmoving chest and breathed it out.

Everything was flowing from her to the boy. Her memories, her rage. All the blood she'd spilled, the sins she'd avenged, and the cries she'd silenced were shaped into shadow, swallowing Mulay's body entirely.

When the darkness faded, giving way to the feeble kerosene light, Anta Sabel's body lay unmoving in the dust. With the woman's eyelids lowered and arms folded atop her chest, it was as if she was sleeping. Freed from her task, Sirabiri had returned to the sweet silence of the grave.

She would never rise again.

* * *

A DEEP, melodic voice hummed from an obscure corner of the tent. There were stars peppered over its owner's exposed ankles, right where the raffia cloth ended. His wooden mask painted with a soft blue, he let a sneer sit on his lips and watched through heavy-lidded eyes.

Mulay flung his eyes open. Slowly, he propelled himself upward, leaving a kiss and a tear on his mother's forehead. As he did, the earth shook from deep within. Mulay lost his balance and fell to the ground. Along with the white man's corpse, dirt-smeared rugs were shoved aside, unveiling a gaping mouth made of wet soil, tree roots, and a churning sea of critters. It swallowed his mother's body and Till's remains. Then, Mulay heard a low sigh, and the earth collapsed in and on itself.

More silent tears fell from his eyes, and he hugged his chest, brushing the unaltered skin where the bullet wound had been. Mulay forced himself up, staring forward. His right eye was a deep black, but the left one was the color of percale.

Sirabiri had left him with a gift, and he was intent on wielding it. The colonizers would pay for all their crimes—both past and present. Mulay trudged away from the tent, glancing over the Europeans' bodies littered all over the camp. With the palm of his hand, he brushed their foreheads, one after the other, and they rose to their feet.

Within the darkness, Taxawaalu chuckled as the Restless followed their new master.

THANK YOU FOR SUPPORTING THE UNDEAD

Tawanna Sullivan
Chandler White
Rhonda Jackson Garcia
Bryan Holm
Kenneth SkaldebÃ¸
Jessica Malitoris
Dave Ring
Suzan Palumbo
Arthur Grauel
Mahogany Rae
Stephanie Shivak
Alysia Cooper
Sarah Macklin
Alexander Danner
Misha Stone
Lee Ann Kostempski
Sean Perry
Andrew Hatchell
Bridget Brave
Holland Dougherty
Regis Donovan
Peregrine Y.
Carol Bailey
Kat Trent

Peter Ong Cook
M'Shai Dash
Allison Kotzig
Ian Mikkelsen
Elsa Ashelford
Cara Murray
Jesse Adams
Alana Joli Abbott
Kelley Frank
Nancy Dunne
Kirsten Kowalewski
Marcia Harris
Ilianna Gonzalez
John Thompson
Adrianna Clark
Christi Nogle
Charles Scogna
Claudia Wair
Erik Dutton
Gale James
David Simerly
NV Haskell
Liese Sherwood-Fabre
Robert Enrico Sohl
Kanari Vivi
Jessica Nettles
Michelle Graf
Pedro Iniguez
D.J. Sylvis
Geoff Sindel
Misty Massey
Kenesha Williams
Rumi Weaver

Gregory Colbert
Akira Sasaki
Julia Smith
Elizabeth Bonesteel
Gaby Triana
Stephanie Cooper
Whitney Trepel
Melanie Loppnow
Elizabeth Wagoner
Paul Cardullo
Jeremiah Taylor
Cedrick May
Ceridwen Christensen
Nathan Williams
Julia Houck
Steven Van Patten
Cathy Keizer
Dawn Landshof
Rachel Brune
Zach Bohannon
Willette Hill
Susan Hance
Rochelle Katz
Nichelle Flentroy
Cindy Stanford
Paula Henderson
eschwanholt
Damoris Tate-Keech
Rodney Holmes
Leekiwi
Brennan Taylor
Jennifer Halbman
Evelyn Thornton

Melanie Hartsfield
Sarah I Jackson
Meg Ward
William Mulligan
Clundoff
Susan Roddey
dinoclaus23
Mrs W J Reynolds
Cathy Green
Candace Wiggins
Ashton Johnson
Keith Gaston
Alicia McCalla
Michael Burke
Ron Dickie
Kevin O'Neill
Sarah Day
Shelley Nash
Maya Preisler
Anya Martin
Melanie C Duncan
Sandor Silverman
Amanda Frederico
Darrell Grizzle
John Grant
Lise Donnelly
Meghan Arcuri-Moran
Nicholas Crook
Gloriknits
Kenya Moss-Dyme
LaShawna Scardina
Michele Berger
Melanie Crew

Carol Gyzander
Sarah Hale
Gary Mitchel
Brad Lile
Elizabeth McClellan
Salem Macknee
Jess Lewis
Christine Crabb
Jl Wheeler-Diggs
Laura V Blackwell
Victoria Fredrick
Joshua Dinges
Amy E Davenport
Allison Charlesworth
Sam Cowan
Scary Stuff Podcast
Joel McCrory
Samantha Bryant
Andrew Hatchell
Dana Cameron
Alana Joli Abbott
Rebekah Hamrick
Chris Hyde
Helen Nde
Nicole Reavis
Aiesha Little
Sean Hillman
Victoria Nations
Creepy podcast
Andrea Thaxton
Sharon Stogner
Donald Kudler
Sumiko Saulson

Marcia Harris
Asiraki
Linda D Addison
Hilary Emmons
Anne Baird

ABOUT THE EDITORS

Nicole Givens Kurtz has been called "a genre polymath who does crime, horror, and SFF (Book Riot)." They've named her as one of the *6 Black SFF Indie Writers You Should be Reading, 30 Must-Read SFF Books by Black Authors,* and *The Best of the West: 8 Alternative History Westerns* (*Sisters of the Wild Sage*). She's a two-time Atomacon Palmetto Scribe Award winner. With over 20 years in publishing, she's written for Pseudopod, Fiyah, Apex Magazine, White Wolf, The Realm (formerly Serial Box), Subsume, and Baen. Nicole has over 50 published short stories and is the author of the *Cybil Lewis* and *Death Violations* cyber-noir series as well as the *Kingdom of Aves* fantasy mystery series. She's written the critically acclaimed, weird western anthology, *Sisters of the Wild Sage: A Weird West Collection.*

Nicole has conducted workshops for Clarion and is an active instructor at Speculative Fiction Academy. She is the owner of Mocha Memoirs Press. She's the editor for the groundbreaking *SLAY: Stories of the Vampire Noire* anthology and co-editor of *Blackened Roots: An Anthology of the Undead.*

Nicole is professional level member of SFWA and HWA. She's represented by Justin Bell at Spectrum Literary Agency.

* * *

Tonia Ransom is the World Fantasy Award-winning creator and executive producer of "NIGHTLIGHT", an IGNYTE Best Fiction Podcast featuring creepy tales written by Black writers, and "Afflicted", a horror thriller best described as Lovecraft Country meets True Blood.

Tonia has been scaring people since the second grade, when she wrote her first story based on Michael Myers. She successfully scared her teacher—just not in the way she intended, but she got hooked on that feeling and the rest is history. She lives in Austin, Texas. You can follow Tonia @missdefying on all the socials. ***Risen*** is her debut book.

ABOUT THE AUTHORS

In Alphabetical Order by Last Name

Marc L Abbott is a Brooklyn native whose work includes The Hooky Party & Etienne and the Stardust Express. He's the co-author of *Hell at Brooklyn Tea* and *Hell at the Way Station,* the two-time African American Literary Award-winning horror anthology. His horror short stories are featured in *Hells Heart, Hells Mall, Even in the Grave,* and the Bram Stoker Nominated horror anthologies *Empire State of Fright; Under Twin Suns: Alternate Histories of the Yellow Sign.* He is a Moth Story Slam and Grand Slam Storyteller winner and an award-winning actor. Find out more about him at www.whoismarclabbott.com.

Milton Davis is an award winning Black Speculative fiction author and owner of MVmedia, LLC, a publishing company specializing in Science Fiction and Fantasy based on African/African Diaspora history, culture, and traditions. Milton is the author of twenty-six novels and short story collections and editor/coeditor of eleven anthologies. His short stories have appeared in several anthologies and magazines, most notably ***Black Panther: Tales of Wakanda, Slay: Stories of the Vampire Noire, Obsidian Literature and Arts in the African Diaspora*** and ***Tales from the Magician's Skull.*** Milton's story 'The Swarm' was nominated for the 2017 British Science Fiction Association Award for Short Fiction and his story, "Carnival", was nominated for the 2020 British Science Fiction Association Award for Short Fiction. He is a recipient of the 2022 East Coast Black Age of Comics Convention Pioneer Lifetime Achievement Award.

Craig Laurance Gidney (he/him/his) is the author of Sea, Swallow Me & Other Stories; Skin Deep Magic: Stories; Bereft (a YA novella), and A Spectral Hue (a novel). He has been a Lambda Literary Finalist three times, was a Carl Brandon Parallax Award Finalist, and won the inaugural Joseph S Pulver Sr Award for Weird Fiction. The Nectar of Nightmares is his most recent collection. He lives in Washington, D.C.

Moustapha Mbacké Diop is a speculative fiction writer from Dakar, Senegal. He studies medicine and is obsessed with African mythology, animation, and horror films. His writing aims to be an exploration of African spirituality, grief, and longing, usually through a darker speculative lens. His work has appeared in Omenana, *the Africa Risen* anthology, and is forthcoming in the *Magazine of Fantasy and Science Fiction.*

Brandon Massey sold his first short story in 1996 to a speculative fiction magazine. Three years later, he self-published *Thunderland,* his first novel. After managing to sell a few thousand copies on his own, Kensington Publishing Corp signed him to a publishing contract and republished the novel in 2002.

Since then, Massey has published up to three books a year, ranging from thriller novels such as *The Landlord* and *The Other Brother,* vampire fiction such as *Dark Corner,* and short story collections such as *Twisted Tales*. Massey currently lives with his family near Atlanta, GA.

Errick Nunnally was born and raised in Boston, Massachusetts, and served one tour in the Marine Corps before deciding art school was a safer pursuit. He enjoys art, comics, and genre novels. A graphic designer, he has trained in Krav Maga and Muay Thai kickboxing. His work has appeared in several anthologies of speculative fiction. His work can be found in APEX MAGAZINE, FIYAH MAGAZINE, GALAXY'S EDGE, LAMPLIGHT, NIGHTLIGHT PODCAST, and the novels, LIGHTNING WEARS A RED CAPE, BLOOD FOR THE SUN, and ALL THE DEAD MEN. Visit errickнunnally.us to learn more about his work.

Eden Royce is a writer from Charleston, SC. She is a Shirley Jackson Award finalist for her short story work and has written articles for Writer's Digest and We Need Diverse Books. Her debut novel *Root Magic* is a Walter Dean Myers Award Honoree, an Andre Norton Nebula Award Finalist, an Ignyte Award winner, and a Mythopoeic Fantasy Award winner for outstanding children's literature. Her second book *Conjure Island* is forthcoming in June 2023. Find her online at http://eden-royce.com.

Steven Van Patten is the author of the celebrated Brookwater's Curse vampire trilogy, and the Killer Genius serial killer series. He's also a co-author of the multiple award-winning Hell at The Way Station, and the sequel Hell at Brooklyn Tea. Numerous

short stories have been published in over a dozen anthologies and he's a contributing writer/consultant for the YouTube channel *Extra History* as well as the star-studded Viral Vignettes series. He's a member of the New York Chapter of The Horror Writer's

Association, The Director's Guild of America, and professional arts fraternity Gamma Xi Phi Incorporated. His website is www.laughingblackvampire.com.

Sumiko Saulson is the Bram Stoker Nominated author of *The Rat King: A Book of Dark Poetry* (*Dooky Zines*), and *Happiness and Other Diseases* (Mocha Memoirs Press); editor of *Black Magic Women: Terrifying Tales by Scary Sisters* (Mocha Memoirs Press). Winner of the Afrosurrealist Writer Award (2018), and Ladies of Horror Fiction Readers Choice Award (2021) They have an AA in English from Berkeley City College, write a column called "Writing While Black" for a national Black Newspaper, the San Francisco BayView, teach courses at the Speculative Fiction Academy, and host the Leather and LGBT Cultural District's "Erotic Storytelling Hour."

L. Marie Wood is a two-time Bram Stoker Award® and Rhysling nominated author, screenwriter, essayist, and poet. She writes high concept fiction that includes elements of psychological horror, mystery, dark fantasy, and romance. Wood is also a MICO Award winner and the founder of the Speculative Fiction Academy, an English and Creative Writing professor, and a horror scholar. Learn more at www.lmariewood.com.

www.ingramcontent.com/pod-product-compliance
Lightning Source LLC
Chambersburg PA
CBHW070630310726
48982CB00001B/236